Savage Rivals
Copyright © 2021 by Becca Steele

All rights reserved. No part of this book may be reproduced or transmitted in any form or by any means, electronic or mechanical, including photocopying, recording or by any information storage and retrieval system, without written permission from the author, except for the use of brief quotations in a book review.

Editing by One Love Editing
Proofreading by Rumi
Cover photography by Michelle Lancaster www.michellelancaster.com
Model: Andy Murray

Becca Steele
www.authorbeccasteele.com

This is a work of fiction. Names, characters, businesses, places, events, locales, and incidents are either the products of the author's crazy imagination or used in a fictitious manner. Any resemblance to actual persons, living or dead, or actual events is purely coincidental.

LEVI vs ASHER

SAVAGE RIVALS

USA TODAY & WALL STREET JOURNAL BESTSELLING AUTHOR
BECCA STEELE

AUTHOR NOTE

The author is British, and this story contains British English spellings and phrases. The football referred to in this story is known as soccer in some countries.

For Kelly

The greatest victory is that which requires no battle.

—Sun Tzu

ONE
ASHER

It hadn't always been this way. The hate that pulsed inside me like a drum, a constant beat that echoed in my head.

Now, it consumed me.

It was all *his* fault.

Levi Woodford.

Number Seven.

"I don't get why you want to do this." Talia, one of my best friends and former on-again, off-again girlfriend, shook her head. "You're just going to make it worse. Can't you call a truce or something?"

"A truce? Are you serious?" Attempting to keep my voice calm, I gave her a rundown of the situation for what felt like the fiftieth fucking time. "You know that Highnam Academy and Alstone High have been football rivals forever. Now that dickhead Seven is captain of Alstone's team, he's trying to throw whatever intimidation tactics he can at me. It's my responsibility as Highnam's team captain to stop him."

"How is offering to fight him in front of a crowd stopping him?" She huffed, annoyed. "Sometimes it feels like I don't even know you, the way you've been obsessing over him lately, since you both started this whole rivalry thing."

"Obsessed? No. It's a matter of pride and showing him that he can't get away with his behaviour." I ignored her muttering, "As if you're any better," and continued. "If I can beat him on *and* off the field, he'll lose respect." I grinned at the thought. "He deserves a fucking beating anyway after what he did last week. Breaking into our school gym and messing with our shit was crossing a major line."

"I can definitely agree with you there." Talia's mouth twisted. "But I really don't like the idea of you fighting him. It's so…uncouth."

"Uncouth, you say? Right."

She studied me, brushing her jaw-length honey-blonde hair out of her eyes as she tilted her head. Attempting to hide her smile, she gave a huge, exaggerated sigh. "Times like this remind me why it never worked out between us. We're too…"

"Different?" I suggested when she seemed to be struggling to find words. She was right, though. We'd been more off than on, our relationship more of a convenience than anything else. Easy, effortless. But Talia was too good for me, too clever, too nice, in all honesty, and she deserved more than what I could give her.

"Different. Yes. We work better as friends, don't we?" She finally let me see the smile pulling at her lips.

I returned it as I stretched, kicking out my legs in front of me. "We argue less when we're friends, that's for sure."

A snort of laughter escaped from her. "That's true. We were never right for each other. What you need is someone as crazy as you, who can handle your unique Asher-ness."

"Asher-ness." I raised a brow. "I hope that's not an insult."

Still smiling, she climbed off my bed and came to stand next to my desk chair, dipping down to kiss the top of my head. "It's not an insult. You know I love you." She sighed. "I just wish you'd listen to me, but I know you never will. You're way too stubborn for that."

Straightening up, she tucked her hair behind her ear, shooting me a concerned glance before heading for my bedroom door. "Don't see me out. Look, I'll be there to cheer you on at the game, okay? I'm on your side, Ash. Always. Just don't let yourself get so caught up in this obsessive rivalry that you lose focus of everything else."

"Thanks, T. I won't." I was lying through my teeth, and Talia knew it. Levi had to answer for what he'd done, and I was going to be the one to make him pay.

Obsessed, she mouthed, slipping out of the door before I could say anything else.

Talia was wrong. I wasn't obsessed with that fucking bastard. I told myself this, even as I found myself driving towards Alstone at 10:00 p.m. My mum was in bed—not that she cared when I was home. Since I'd turned eighteen, she'd told me that now I was an adult, I could do whatever I wanted. Like I hadn't been doing that already. My deadbeat dad hadn't been on the scene since I was six, so I had no one to answer to, other than my nosy as fuck friends.

But this was my secret. Gathering intel. *Not* obsession.

There was a difference.

The thirty-minute drive passed in no time, and soon I was pulling into a space at the side of the road just outside Parton Park, two hundred acres of parkland and sports facilities, including a skate park with ramps and pipes, and a long wall behind it, covered in colourful graffiti.

The skate park was my destination.

Drawing my hood up to shadow my face, I jogged towards the crowds surrounding the massive, scooped-out bowl that was normally full of skaters, except on nights like this. Sunday nights. Fight nights.

Fight nights and football games were the only times when Alstone High School and Highnam Academy were on a level playing field. The rest of the time, they acted like they were too good for the rest of us. Just because they were rich, spoilt brats used to having whatever money could buy. You had to pay to go to school at Alstone High, for fuck's sake, and the annual fees alone were more than my mum made in a year working full-time at the supermarket warehouse. As far as I was concerned, education was a right, not a privilege.

Last year hadn't been quite so bad. Carter Blackthorne had been captain of the Alstone High football team, and he'd been alright. A fair player and a decent fighter—he and his best mate, Kian, had won more fights at the bowl than anyone else. He hadn't been interested in our rivalry outside the football field, and that was fine by me.

This year, everything had changed.

Carter had graduated, gone to university, and in his place there was a new captain.

Levison Woodford, known as Levi to almost everyone.

I called him Seven, after his football number.

The bastard started it first. Calling me "Ten" the very

first time we'd played against each other in a preseason "friendly" match, sneering out the word as if it was an insult. Well, fuck him, because I was proud of that number on my football shirt.

All because I'd refused to shake his hand in the prematch ritual, and I'd only done that because of the look he'd given me. A condescending, disdainful look, like he thought I was scum. Beneath him in every way. Like I wasn't even worthy enough to be breathing the same air as him. Shouldn't have expected any less from someone who had parents that thought Levison was a good name for a kid.

Things had gone downhill after that point. We'd been on each other's heels the whole match, right up until the eighty-third minute. My best friend and teammate, Danny, got tackled and dived, playing up his injury, and the referee had ruled in our favour, giving the Alstone High player a red card and us a penalty.

After that minute, Levi had been out for blood. I'd hold my hands up and admit that I hadn't helped the situation by gloating, but we'd both earned yellow cards from our purposeful tackles against one other. By the time the final whistle blew and the game ended in a 1-0 win for Highnam Academy, both of us were completely fucking wound up, and if the game had gone on any longer, I know we both would have ended up being sent off the pitch with red cards.

It had only got worse since then, starting with taunts on social media and escalating to last week's vandalism of our school property by the AHS players. That had been the final straw.

So I'd put my plan into place, and it was time to begin.

Making my way through the crowds surrounding the bowl, I kept my face lowered, choosing to remain anonymous. I'd timed it just right. Standing with my hands in my pockets, behind a couple of girls sitting on the lip of the bowl, I stared down to see Levi circling another guy in the pit.

His normally impeccably styled ash-brown hair was mussed and falling into his eyes, and instead of his perfectly pressed clothes, he was wearing jeans that hung low on his hips and no top.

I sucked my lip between my teeth, studying him for weaknesses that I could exploit. I hadn't been expecting him to be so…defined. He was deceptively lean with clothes on, but even from where I was standing, I could see his muscles flexing, so taut and hard, his body coiled tight, waiting to spring on his opponent. Everything about him was harsh lines and angles, and his silver eyes were cold. If it hadn't been for those long, blond-tipped lashes and his soft, full lips, he would—

Hold the fuck up. I gave myself an internal shake. Levi's face wasn't important, other than the fact that I'd like to mar it with a few bruises. And hopefully I'd be getting the chance, sooner rather than later.

As the fight started, I watched intently, looking out for any moves he favoured or any tells that would give me an advantage when it came to me fighting him. When the whistle blew and the referee held Levi's hand up, announcing him as the winner, I couldn't even find it in myself to be irritated by his smug, arrogant smile, my mind too busy cataloguing every move he'd made. He favoured his left side, and he always dropped his fist right before he hit his opponent with a right hook. It could be something that would give me an advantage, and I was going to need it. Despite the fact that I could hold my own, this fucker was good. Better than good.

I needed to face him in the bowl. And there was no way I was going to let him win.

Slipping away from the crowds, I moved on to the second part of tonight's mission and settled down to wait.

"Nice fight."

Levi threw me his usual disdainful look, seemingly unsurprised to see me. "Following me, Ten? I suppose I should be flattered, but...it's you. Move away from my car, now, before you contaminate it."

I remained where I was, leaning against the side of his rich-boy car—an orange-and-black McLaren 540C—with my arms folded across my chest. "Nah, I don't think I will."

His grey eyes flashed, his lip curling into a sneer, and I smiled. Getting a rise out of the person I hated more than anyone else was so satisfying.

"What do you want?" he finally asked in a clipped voice when it was clear that I wasn't going anywhere.

"Does your daddy know that his precious boy likes to get his hands dirty at the bowl?"

I could hear him grinding his teeth, his hands fisting at his sides. "You can leave now."

"Why would I do that?" Pushing off his car, I drew myself up to my full height. Unfortunately, I was only slightly taller than him, but it still counted in my opinion. "Don't you want to talk to me?"

"What makes you think I'd have anything I wanted to say to you?" He stepped forwards, his chest brushing against mine, and the image of his toned torso flashed through my mind, completely without warning.

"You. Me. Fight," I ground out, suddenly flustered.

"Don't they teach you how to speak in full sentences at

Highnam Academy?"

"Shut the fuck up, Seven." I pushed against him, knocking him off balance. His arm flew out, his long fingers gripping my bicep and digging in. He immediately released me as if he'd been burned, a noise that sounded like a growl coming from his throat.

Regaining my composure, I leaned back against his car. "Bit growly for a posh boy, aren't you?"

Levi's reply was to bare his teeth at me. "You're the one who can't speak in full fucking sentences."

"He swears, too. Maybe I *am* a bad influence," I mused, watching his grey eyes darken, the tips of his ears turning red as he stared at me as if he was trying to incinerate me with his eyes. "Better stop that before you burst a blood vessel."

When the punch came, I was prepared, but I still staggered back against his car with the force of the blow. Still, I smiled as I wheezed out a breath, because it meant I'd managed to make him lose his cool, to get under his skin.

"You're nothing but Highnam scum. A bully with not even two brain cells to rub together, on a loser team. Your little world is so sad that you have to try and provoke me just to make your pathetic life feel a bit better." The contempt in his eyes froze me in place. "Tell me, Ten. Does it make you feel good to come here and—"

"Fucking shut *up*!" Shoving at him, I knew I'd properly lost my composure this time, but somehow he'd managed to push my buttons, and now I was just as angry as he was. "You brought this on yourself. If you hadn't been such an asshole in the first place, maybe things wouldn't have escalated."

"*Me*?" The shock in his tone was clear. Like I'd expect

anything less. He'd never take the blame for anything.

"Yes. *You*. I say we work this shit out once and for all, in the bowl. Pick a date, and we'll make it happen."

Silence fell.

"I'm not fighting you." The anger went out of his tone, and a mask slipped into place, his features blank. "Now get away from my car. I've had enough of slumming it for one evening."

"What's the matter? Too scared to fight me?"

"Yeah. So scared." He shoved me aside, which I wasn't expecting, and dived into his car, locking the doors behind him.

I jumped back as the engine started up with a roar, and all I could do was throw up my middle fingers as he left me for dust with the sound of revving engines and squealing tyres echoing in my ears.

TWO
ASHER

"Have you seen this?" Danny, my football teammate and closest friend aside from Talia, shoved his phone under my nose. I pushed my dark hair out of my eyes, frowning at the screen.

"The papers just fucking love them, don't they?" A bitter laugh juddered out of me as I studied the image and accompanying article on the local newspaper website. There was a huge photo of the Alstone High School football team, all poised, smugly grinning camaraderie, posed on their perfectly manicured football pitch, with the honey-coloured stone buildings of their school in the background. Their captain stood front and centre, and he was the only one not smiling, staring at the camera with a challenge in his eyes.

He taunted me through the screen. Fucking Levi. The need to take him on in the bowl was like a constant itch under my skin that I couldn't get rid of. Why wouldn't he fight me? He hadn't been shy about punching me in the stomach last night by his car. Good thing he'd been standing too close to get any power behind the punch. When we fought, I wanted witnesses. I wanted everyone to see me take down Alstone High's king.

"The papers might love them, but that means fuck all. We can take them." Danny gave me a sly sideways look. "If you can control your obsession with their captain and act like a team player."

I shot him a warning look, and he smirked at me. Shoving at his arm, I pushed through the school gates and onto the grounds of Highnam Academy. As a car passed us, followed by a group on mopeds, pulling into the small car park to the right of the school, I felt a momentary twinge of frustration that I had to walk here. But my Honda Civic Type R was the only possession I owned that had any value, and the way things went in this school? If I parked it here, by the end of the day, it would be trashed.

We entered through the sliding doors and joined the queue of students waiting to be scanned by security. Up ahead, a guy from one of my classes was having a knuckle duster confiscated. Amateur. If you wanted to bring weapons into school, you didn't just stroll in through the front entrance with them on your person. You used the side door, the one that was never checked, that led into the technology block.

The sandy-haired, beefy security guy swept the wand scanner over me absently, probably bored to death with the mindless routine. "Alright, mate?" I saluted him with a grin, and he responded with an eye roll. One of these days, I'd get him to crack.

"You can't confiscate that—it's my grandad's letter opener! It's a family heirloom!" Danny's voice came from behind me, and I turned back around to see what was happening. The security guy was holding up a small, slim knife, shiny and wicked-looking.

"This." He held it between two fingers, shaking his head. "This is not a letter opener, Mr. Jones, nor is it an heirloom. Now go, before I report this to the head. You're already three points away from suspension, if I remember correctly. Wouldn't want you to miss the match on Saturday."

The match against Alstone High School. That was why the security guy was turning a blind eye. Some things were a matter of pride, and if there was one thing that could unite the school, it was the desire to put AHS in their place on the field.

Danny caught up with me. "Can't believe he confiscated my knife."

"You're a dickhead," I told him as we headed towards our lockers. "Why didn't you use the side entrance?"

He shrugged. "Dunno. Forgot."

Talia strutted up to us, effectively ending the conversation. "Who's ready to learn about anatomy?"

"I'm ready to learn about your anatomy." Danny leered at her, and she elbowed him in the stomach.

"Your lines get worse all the time." Swinging her locker open, she pulled out a heavy textbook. "Carry this for me."

I raised a brow as he silently took the book from her. He caught my look and threw me a wink. "Gotta keep them sweet." Turning to Talia, he shifted his bag onto one shoulder, tucking her book under his arm. "T, are you free tonight?"

"I'm busy."

"That's what you always say. I'll wear you down one of these days."

Shaking my head at them, I grabbed my own book from my locker, and we made our way to the science labs for our sports science class—current module: anatomy. Since I'd told Danny that there was a zero percent chance of me and Talia getting back together, he'd taken it as a green light to try and get her to go out with him. So far, she'd knocked him back at every opportunity, but both of them seemed to enjoy this little game they were playing, and it amused me to watch. I had no romantic feelings for Talia anymore, but I felt protective of her, so as far as I was concerned, having her and my best mate together was an ideal outcome. Better that than some Alstone High poser. I'd seen the way the boys had eyed her when we'd been around them. A lot of them acted like all Highnam Academy girls were easy, willing to spread their legs for the rich boys who deigned to pay them a bit of attention.

Okay, I guess that some of the girls were like that. But Talia wasn't.

Levi better not think about trying it on with her.

"I bet I can guess what you're thinking about."

"Huh?" My head shot up, and I realised I'd zoned out. We were already sitting in the classroom, and Danny was smirking at me with a knowing glint in his pale blue eyes.

"You've got that look on your face. Like you've eaten something really nasty." He pulled a face, which I really fucking hoped didn't look like mine. "You get it whenever you think about that asshole, Levi."

"Yeah." I didn't even deny it. "Did I tell you he refused to fight me at the bowl?"

"What?" Rubbing his hand over his close-cropped, light brown hair, he frowned. "He's probably scared. Doesn't want to lose face in front of everyone."

"What are we talking about?" Talia leaned over the lab table.

"Levi won't fight Ash. Craven bastard."

Resting my elbows on the table, I tapped my fingers against the chipped surface, amused. "Craven? Have you been watching medieval shit again, Dan?"

"I told you it was a bad idea in the first place," Talia reminded me. "He—"

"Quiet!" The booming voice of Mr. Allen came from the front of the classroom, and we fell silent, but a glance from Danny told me that the conversation was far from over.

When the after-school football training was over, I gathered my teammates outside the gym before everyone disappeared to shower and change. "Good session. We can easily kick Alstone's ass on Saturday if we play like we did today." When everyone stared at me expectantly, I added, "And payback is coming for what they did to our gym."

That got a reaction. Everyone wanted retribution, and it was coming. Levi and his friends thought they were untouchable, but we were going to prove them wrong.

They wouldn't even see it coming.

Heading into the gym, I stared around me, my anger building as I recalled the destruction that Alstone High had been responsible for. They'd trashed our changing rooms—damaging our lockers, tampering with the gym equipment, and worst of all, they'd got hold of our second set of uniforms and coated them in oil. Nothing could get it out. And we didn't exactly have bags of cash to replace the ruined kit.

They hadn't left anything incriminating, other than one thing. A number seven, spray-painted in black on my personal locker—the one in the centre of the room with my name and number chalked on it.

Yeah, it was a message for me, from their team captain. A message I received loud and clear.

Revenge would be sweet.

"I can't believe they were such bad losers that they trashed our gym." Omar, our goalie, bashed at his open locker door with his knuckles, attempting to knock out the dent without any success.

Danny looked up from his position on the bench, where he was unlacing his boots. "I can. Bellends."

Omar slammed his locker door shut. "Fucking wankers. They're going to get what's coming to them."

"They will," I assured him. "First, we have to get through this match and win it. After that...we plan."

My phone beeped from inside my locker, interrupting my train of thought. "I've gotta go. I'm going to be late for work." Yanking my sweaty football kit off, I jogged across to the showers, steeling myself as freezing cold water hit my skin. They took forever to warm up, and I didn't have time to wait around. I couldn't afford to lose my job.

As far as jobs went, it wasn't anything to boast about. Stacking shelves in the convenience store near my house for three evenings a week, it barely paid the minimum wage, but the money was enough to keep my car running and put aside a tiny amount for the future. I still didn't know what I was going to do, but I didn't want to stay in Highnam for any longer than I had to. A former seaside resort, back in the days when people didn't go abroad for their holidays, it was now a dead-end town with zero prospects. Exactly how Alstone would have been if it didn't have rich families pumping cash into it.

Once I was back at home, I dumped my bag and grabbed the navy polo shirt that was my work uniform, throwing it on with a pair of jeans and a hoodie. I poked my head into the lounge, where my mum was asleep in front of the TV, napping after her twelve-hour shift. Picking up the blanket that was draped over the back of the sofa, I covered her and turned the TV down low. Then I let myself out of the house.

"I saved you a Cornish pasty and a packet of crisps," Selina, my supervisor, told me as soon as I walked through the door. "They're out the back."

"You're the best," I told her, and she smiled.

"Don't forget it."

Making my way to the back of the shop, I entered the stockroom. There were floor-to-ceiling racks alongside fridges and freezers where all the stock was stored, and at the back was a roll-up door where the vans delivered the goods. In one corner, we had a table and two chairs and a tiny counter with a sink, microwave, and kettle. There was a door leading to a small toilet, and that was essentially it. Nothing to get excited about. I put the pasty in the microwave to warm it up, then opened the crisps. This was one of the upsides of my job. There was always food going to waste, so the staff could help themselves to anything that was due to go out of date that no one had bought. Since my mum was often working or asleep during usual dinner hours, this was a convenient way for me to eat when I didn't have time to cook.

After wolfing down my food, washed down by a glass of water, I set to work, walking back through the store and checking which supplies were low before returning to the stockroom to grab the necessary supplies. I put my earphones in and switched off, stacking the shelves on autopilot, then moving on to wiping down the fridges and freezers. The four-hour shift passed quickly, and the second it hit 10:00 p.m., Selina locked the doors. We closed everything up, and I saw her to her house. She lived directly opposite the small row of shops, but even so, I didn't want her walking on her own at night.

Once she was safely inside her house, I turned and headed for the alleyway that was a cut-through to my road, pulling my hood up as I set a fast pace through the dark passageway.

"Well, well, well. Looks like I caught myself a Highnam rat."

Someone yanked at my hoodie, pulling me back.

Too bad for them, I was already prepared. I let myself be pulled, though, recognising the voice. If he thought he had an advantage over me, he was sorely mistaken.

He mouthed off for a minute or two longer before he finally paused for breath. While he'd been talking, I'd used the time to dig into my pocket, and now, it was time to give him a little scare of his own.

"Milo." Easily moving out of his hold, I gripped him so he was immobile and pressed my knife to his throat, the flat of the blade against his skin. "Meet Ruby."

Predictably, he instantly stilled. Levi's best friend thought he could get the better of me, but he was completely clueless. "Want to tell me what you're doing here? Oh, wait. I know." Without giving him a chance to speak, I continued.

"You're here to top up your weed supply, am I right? Or are you running low on pills? We're not good enough for you to be seen with, but we're good enough to take your drug money, aren't we?"

"W-who's Ruby?" he stammered.

I lifted the knife away from his neck and held it up. "Ruby." I didn't bother explaining how Talia had named my red-bladed knife as a joke when I'd first got it, and it had kind of stuck.

It wasn't that I *wanted* to carry a knife around with me, but around here, you could never be too careful. And with the number of people who did carry them? Let's just say you wouldn't want to be caught out if someone came at you with a knife and you had no way to defend yourself.

That was just the way things were. Don't get me wrong, Highnam wasn't a hotbed of crime or anything. But it was wise to take precautions.

"Run along now. Wouldn't want anything to happen to you in this dark, dark alley." Lowering my voice, I purred the words in his ear, satisfied as he flinched away from me. I released him, and he disappeared as quickly as he could.

Hopefully, word of this little interaction with Milo would make its way back to Levi. A warning not to mess with me.

Safely stowing my knife away, I dug my hands into my hoodie pockets to keep them warm, then made my way home.

THREE
ASHER

Glancing in the rear-view mirror, I indicated to turn right into the grounds of Alstone High School. Right behind me was the minibus carrying the rest of the football team, but while I navigated in the direction of the student car park, they turned into the visitor parking area.

Technically, I should've parked there, too, but I happened to know for a fact that a certain eighteen-year-old football captain parked his very expensive, very flashy car in the prime spot in the student car park, closest to the school entrance, and no one else was allowed to park next to him in case they damaged his precious car.

A fact I was about to take advantage of.

Navigating into the space next to Levi's driver-side door, I purposely parked at an angle, ensuring he wouldn't be able to open his door unless I moved.

"Ash, seriously. Do you have to?" Talia crawled over the centre console, and I helped her out of the car since she couldn't get out of the passenger door, thanks to my stellar parking skills. Once she was out, I angled my seat forwards so Danny could climb out of the back.

"Of course he does. And just so you know, I'm going in the front on the way back. My legs are too long for that back seat." Danny stretched, groaning.

Talia raised a brow. "We'll see."

"Maybe I could be persuaded…"

I left them to their little flirting game, opening the boot and pulling out Danny's and my gym bags before locking the car. My mind turned to the game—there'd be time to fuck with Levi afterwards. Now, I had to make sure that our team won.

"Come on. We've got a match to win." I made for the visitors' car park to meet up with the rest of the team and the two staff members that were there to supervise. One was Mr. Matthews "call me Dave," one of the school PE teachers, and the other was Mick Shaw, a guy on Highnam Academy's board of governors, who used to be a semi-professional footballer. Mick had been instrumental in our success the last year or so, giving us tips and tricks he'd picked up in his days in the Arsenal youth team and then as a semi-pro player.

We trailed into the visitor changing room, stowing our bags and changing into our football kits. Dave and Mick talked the whole time, last-minute words of advice and encouragement.

Then it was time.

As we filed out onto the football pitch, the heavy atmosphere hit me. There was normally a sense of rivalry at our games, but this was different. The Alstone High stands were swamped with fans in black and green, the AHS team colours, far outnumbering our own blue and white. And they were baying for blood.

"Fucking hell," Danny muttered to me. "The crowd's a bit riled up today."

Cocking my head, I listened to the shouts, a constant roar that filled the stadium. "Yeah, I guess they took offence at our win in the last game."

If I admitted it to myself, our win had been helped by Danny diving and completely playing up the injury that had got their player sent off the pitch with a red card. My resulting penalty had sealed our win, and I'd wasted no time gloating in Levi's face.

It was the way things were. I knew he'd do the same if his team had been in our position.

The referee held up the coin as our team faced AHS. Grey eyes met mine, stormy and defiant.

You're going down, I mouthed as Levi replied to the ref while he kept his gaze fixed on mine, his jaw tense and his fists clenched.

Fuck you, Ten, he mouthed back as the referee flipped the coin.

"Heads it is. Alstone High kick off," the ref announced, interrupting Levi's and my staring contest.

A huge cheer went up from the stands, and the second Milo touched the ball, I was hit with the certainty that we'd completely miscalculated our strategy.

The crowd wanted blood, and the AHS team were playing to win.

Danny got taken down by a vicious tackle, calculated for maximum effect when the referee was distracted by a commotion at the other end of the pitch. Outraged and protesting about the dirty tactics, our right-winger ended up getting into an altercation with one of the AHS players and got a red card, putting him out of the match.

Down one player, our fate was sealed, and we didn't even have a chance.

The Alstone High team got their first opportunity at a goal from a free kick that the referee had awarded, thanks to my frustration spilling over and miscalculating a tackle on one of their players.

"I thought a team captain was supposed to lead by example?" Levi elbowed me as he passed, out of sight of the ref. "Need some pointers on how to play?"

It took everything in me not to punch his smug face, and I only stopped myself because I knew he was trying to get in my head, to make me snap and get sent off the pitch. "Fuck you, Seven," I snarled. "Stay out of my way."

When AHS inevitably scored, the crowd went fucking crazy, and I could tell that it was affecting my teammates. We were fucked from the beginning, and every single thing that went against us in this match was another nail in the coffin.

In the end, the Alstone High team didn't just win, they annihilated us, 4-0.

At the end of the match, we limped off the pitch to the sound of boos and jeers and suffered through a severe dressing-down by Dave and Mick. We deserved it. We'd fallen apart. I didn't know where or how it had all gone so wrong, but as the team captain, I got the worst of it.

My mood still low, I fumbled my way through a pep talk in an attempt to bolster everyone's mood, which was a complete failure since we were all gutted about the loss. Then I left the rest of my teammates at the minibus and went to stand with Danny at the edge of the car park, waiting for Talia.

"Well, that was a complete shitshow," Danny muttered, kicking at the ground.

"Yeah." There was nothing else to say.

Talia appeared from around the corner of the school building and immediately pulled me into a hug, then hugged Danny. I could tell how low he was feeling by the fact that he didn't even attempt to ask her out, and she picked up on it straight away, shooting me a look over his shoulder. Giving her a nod, I stepped back, and her mouth curved into a small smile.

"You're not even going to ask me out today?" Drawing back, she stared at Danny.

He shook his head.

"That's a shame, because I was thinking of saying yes this time."

"What?" It was like he had a sudden personality transformation. "Now? Let's go." Gripping her hand, he began tugging her in the direction of the road. She laughed, going along with him.

He stopped, turning back to me. "Will—"

"Go," I said. "Text me later." Spinning on my heel, I headed in the direction of my car. They didn't need me there, and at this point in time, I just wanted to be alone, to lick my wounds in private.

I'd forgotten how I'd parked my car.

I was greeted by Levi, cold and furious. "Move your piece of shit car, now."

All the disappointment and rage that I'd been holding back spilled out of me as I stalked up to him, pushing my chest into his. "No."

"Move it."

"*No*."

He bared his teeth in a snarl, and I loved that I could get a reaction out of him. This bastard was going down.

"Gonna fight me in the bowl? Or are you too scared?"

"You're a loser, on and off the field," he spat through gritted teeth. "You should be the one who's scared."

"Yeah?" In a flash, I had him pinned against my car, wrapping my hand around his throat. His pulse thundered under my grip, but he didn't even flinch. Leaning forwards, I spoke into his ear, low and threatening. "And yet I'm the one pinning you down."

"So you think."

Before I had time to process what was happening, Levi had broken out of my hold and spun me around, pushing me face down against my own car, my back to his chest, and his hand around my throat in a tight, punishing grip.

"You were saying?" The anger had disappeared from his tone, and now he almost sounded amused.

I hated him.

Fortunately for me, I had plenty of tricks up my sleeve. Using a sneaky manoeuvre I'd picked up from my cousin, I twisted down and around, freeing my arms and getting them around him in a grappling move.

"I was saying." Tightening my grip, I pressed into him. A low noise came from his throat, his breath hitting the side of my face in harsh, quick pants. "I'm the one pinning you down." Technically, I wasn't pinning him, but semantics.

This was actually fun. As much as I couldn't stand him, he didn't let me push him around. He stood up to me, didn't let me bully him.

We grappled with each other, both trying to gain the upper hand, before his foot caught around my ankle, tripping me and sending me sprawling to the ground. I hit the tarmac hard.

"Move your car, *now*." His foot connected with my ribs, knocking the breath from my lungs.

Gasping, I rolled away from him and sprung to my feet. I launched myself at him, sending us both crashing into his car. Our heads smacked together, and I pulled away with a wince. This wasn't going to end well, and I needed to regroup.

"Okay. Fuck, Seven. Why do you have to be such an asshole?" I growled at him, and he shot me a glare.

"Move your car, or I'll have you locked in this car park and get your car towed for illegal parking. Do you want that to happen?"

Typical rich boy, using his status to get his way.

Turning my back on him, I yanked my keys from my pocket and stalked around the side of my car. After sliding into my seat and gunning the engine, I reversed out of the space, pulling alongside Levi, who was still watching me with that intense glare fixed on his face, his powerful, lean body tensed, ready to spring into action if I tried anything else. "This isn't over yet." Flipping him a finger, I pulled out of the car park.

The last thing I saw in my rear-view mirror was him slumped against the side of his car with his head in his hands.

FOUR
LEVI

"You know that Highnam are going to want payback. Doubly so, after what we did to their school, and now with us kicking their asses on the football pitch." My best friend, Milo, hit a combination of buttons on his PS5 controller, making his character leap in the air and rain fire down on mine.

"How did you manage to kill me again," I muttered, watching my character's health bar deplete to zero. "I know they're going to want payback, but we'll be ready for them."

Milo rocked back in the gaming chair, one of two in the media room we were currently occupying. It was my favourite place in my house—huge sofas, dim lighting, all the gaming equipment I needed, and a giant TV with surround sound. Soundproofed, too, which had actually been for my parents' benefit, since they didn't want to have to hear the sounds from the speakers booming through the house.

"They won't be able to break into our school, at least.

They're way too dumb to get past the security," he asserted, loading up a new game. "I want to try that new arena we unlocked. Want to switch to another character?"

"No, I'll stick with the same." My mind was only half on the conversation, and the rest was on something else.

Some*one* else, to be precise. Asher Henderson, the bane of my existence. Dark hair, dark eyes, his body all defined lines and sculpted muscles, he was way too good-looking considering he took zero care with his appearance. And he knew he looked good, based on the cocky expression that was permanently affixed to his face, making me want to punch him every time I saw him.

"Who does Ten think he is, anyway? I can't believe he tried blocking my car in." My jaw clenched. I didn't normally have an anger problem, but Asher got under my skin like nothing else. Even now, just picturing his face was enough to sour my mood.

"He's just trying to get in your head, to throw you off your game. Just rise above it." Milo paused the game. "Want a drink?" Before I could reply, he climbed to his feet, dragging his hand through his black hair as he stretched, yawning. He headed over to the mini fridge in the corner of the room and pulled out two cans of Coke, before returning to me. We'd grown up together, and he practically lived at my house. As did most of the football team, come to think of it, and their girlfriends, including Katie, Milo's girlfriend. They'd been together for almost three months now, and it was the longest relationship he'd been in. In fact... I glanced at my watch. Everyone was due here in around twenty minutes so we could have a planning meeting.

Yeah, a planning meeting. Halloween was coming up, and it had been decided, *not* by me, that the football team needed to continue with tradition. A tradition that had only begun last October, when the county council decided to put on a huge Halloween event in Parton Park that they called "Fright Night." It was essentially a giant funfair, with music and entertainment, open to everyone in the surrounding areas. Unfortunately for me, that included the students of Highnam Academy.

Last year, Carter, the captain of the Alstone High football team, and two of his friends had organised a game for Fright Night. The objective was to pull pranks without being caught and upload the evidence to a server, where the winner would be decided. They also had a thing with chasing girls and capturing them to take them to a private after-party, although I wasn't sure how that related to the game. Anyway, during the event they'd all worn Purge-style neon masks to hide their identities, and the game and after-party had been so popular that it had been decided that the football team would organise something along the same lines this year.

Which meant me, although, I got to leave the actual planning to Milo and Katie, since they'd offered to take it on. My job was mostly to approve or veto suggestions.

"...He's dangerous. I think you should stay away from him."

"Huh?" I blinked, returning to the present. "Sorry. I was thinking about Fright Night. What were you saying?"

Milo rolled his eyes, tapping at his controller. "I said, you should stay away from Asher—don't piss him off. I know you can't help it, but he's dangerous."

"Dangerous, how?" I was barely even looking at the screen at this point, mashing the buttons on my controller and randomly doing a jump-kick combo that knocked

Milo's character out.

"Don't tell anyone, but…" He took a deep breath, and I gave up on trying to focus on the game, giving him my full attention. Throwing his controller down, he rubbed his hand across his face. "I was in Highnam the other night, getting more weed from my supplier. I saw Asher through a shop window as I was driving past, and I…fuck, this is embarrassing."

"Just tell me."

He groaned but nodded. "Okay, so I pulled over, thinking it would be fun to mess with him. He was helping a woman lock up the shop—I guess he works there or something—and then when she'd gone, he started walking off down this dodgy alleyway. I managed to sneak up behind him and grab him, but then he pulled a knife on me! An actual proper sharp knife! Who the fuck does that, Levi?" His voice cracked, just barely, but I noticed it. The whole thing had clearly unnerved him. "It might sound dramatic, but I honestly thought he was going to stab me at one point. That guy is a psycho."

"He threatened you with a knife?"

"Yes."

"You shouldn't have been following him down a dark alley," I pointed out.

"Huh? Why are you sticking up for him? I thought you were on my side." Milo pursed his lips, shaking his head. "Sometimes I wonder if you really hate him or if all this is some kind of fucked-up foreplay."

"*What*?" I recoiled, throwing my head back against the back of the chair. "Why would you even—fuck! That's just so—"

"Yeah, okay. I didn't mean it." The sideways glance he

gave me told me that he didn't believe his own words. "It's just...you're a bit obsessed with him."

"Because he's the bane of my life. Believe me, I'd like nothing more than for him to disappear for good. My life was great until he showed up as Highnam's football captain, and now I have a permanent tension headache from dealing with his shit."

Milo stretched his legs out in front of him, his brow furrowed. "We probably shouldn't have done what we did to their gym, should we?"

"Probably not, but it's too late for regrets." I sighed. "We just have to make sure we're prepared for whatever form of retaliation they decide to take."

My phone chimed with an alert, and I hit the doorbell app to let the rest of the football team into the house. "Enough about that now. Tell me what you're planning for Fright Night."

―――

Two hours later, and the restless feeling inside of me that had been there ever since Milo told me about his interaction with Asher was getting worse.

Climbing to my feet, I turned to Milo, sprawled on the sofa with his girlfriend. "I'm heading out. Lock up when you leave?"

He nodded, not questioning me, which I appreciated. He had his own key and knew all the security codes to my house, and it wasn't unusual for him to be here even when I wasn't. His parents were close friends of mine, and my parents encouraged him (and all our other friends, for that matter) to come over as often as possible, always keeping the house stocked with plenty of supplies for our huge appetites. I think it made them feel better about working such long hours and leaving me to my own devices.

Before I could get waylaid by anyone else, I headed out of the media room and through the house to the garage. I stopped, thinking for a minute. My McLaren would get way too much attention in Highnam, so I swiped the keys for the black Range Rover that my dad hardly ever used. At least it wasn't orange, so it would blend in.

Then, I set off towards Highnam.

I didn't even have a real plan in mind, but gathering information on my rival was wise, and a warning to stay away from Milo wouldn't go amiss, either. I knew where Milo's supplier lived since I'd been there a number of times with him, so I had an idea of which shop he'd been referring to. I hadn't asked him for more details, though. Making him suspicious, when he already had some weird idea that I was obsessed with Asher...bad idea.

When I pulled up in one of the parking spaces in front of the small row of shops, I sat and waited for a few minutes. Most of the shopfronts were dark and shuttered, except for a Chinese takeaway on the far left, and right in front of me, a small convenience store.

A figure emerged from between the shelves, and I got out of the car.

In five steps, I was at the shop door, cataloguing the space inside before I entered. The till was over to the left, with a pretty woman with a dark brown ponytail sitting behind it. Asher had his back to me, reaching up to place some packets up on one of the high shelves. His faded, ripped jeans hugged his legs perfectly, and his too-tight polo shirt stretched across his back, showing those powerful muscles. As usual, his hair was a fucking mess, short at the back and sides, but a mop of soft brown strands lying every which way on top. Hadn't he ever heard of hair product? Or a brush, for that matter?

When someone cleared their throat behind me, I startled, realising I'd been blocking the doorway while I watched Asher. "Sorry, mate." I stepped aside, letting the teenage boy in before resuming my perusal of the shop. Asher finished loading the packets on the shelf, then crouched down to do up the trailing laces on his battered Nikes before straightening up and making his way towards the back of the shop, where I could see a door that presumably led to the stockroom.

It was time to make my move. I had no real plan, but I needed to confront him, to see that rage appear, making his brown eyes flash with anger, all fire and fury.

He riled me up without even trying, so it was only fair that I did the same to him.

Entering the shop, I moved between the shelves, thankful for the teenage boy who was currently occupying the attention of the girl on the till, attempting to buy a two-litre bottle of cider, even though he was clearly under eighteen.

Asher appeared in the back doorway again, and I ducked around the end of the aisle, coming around behind him.

"Ten." I pressed my body against his back, my arms braced on the shelves either side of him, caging him in.

He cursed, dropping the box he was holding, his whole body stiffening. "Stalking me now, are you?" The anger in his voice was unmistakable.

Angling my head forwards, I put my mouth to his ear. The scent of his aftershave hit me, a subtle, woodsy smell.

"Who are you wearing aftershave for?"

Fuck. That was *not* what I meant to say, at all.

"Wouldn't you like to know?" His voice turned low and husky, and my brain went offline. It was the only explanation for my reaction.

"Yes, I would." My lips brushed against his ear, and his sharp intake of breath was loud in the absolute silence.

My own breaths came quicker, heavier, and I had to force my body to take a step back, to drop my arms to my sides. As soon as I moved, the spell was broken and he spun around, fire in his eyes. "What the hell are you doing here, stalking me in my workplace? I can't afford to lose this job, dickhead."

There was real worry beneath the fire, which I'd never once seen from him before, and it took me aback. Something inside me twisted. I took another step away from him, holding up my hands. "I wasn't coming here to get you fired, so relax."

"Relax around *you*? You're a fucking snake, ready to strike when I least expect it."

"Yeah? If I'm a snake, what does that make you?" I spat.

He pulled his lip between his teeth, thinking, and I had to tear my gaze away from him. "A bigger snake," he said eventually, "so you'd better watch your back. Whatever your game is, you won't win."

"Why did you threaten my best friend with a knife?" I managed to force out the question that I'd originally intended to ask him, the anger rising in me again as I thought of what he'd done. Milo had been thoughtless and acted rashly, chasing Asher down an alley at night, but that didn't excuse what Asher had done. My anger rose even further, ready to boil over, my fists clenching and my jaw tightening. "You could've seriously hurt him, and carrying a knife is illegal."

"I don't see any police around. And since you're so interested in my knife..." He moved so fast, I didn't even have time to react, yanking me to him and pushing me through the door into the storeroom. Holding me against the wall with his arm across my chest, he did something with his other hand, and the next second, a long, wicked-looking knife with a blood-red blade was being held in my face. "Here's Ruby."

What the fuck? I held myself completely still. Asher could be volatile, and I didn't want to provoke him while he had the knife out.

It took an effort to keep my voice measured, to stop the rage bleeding through my tone. "Why are you doing this?"

"Why am I doing what, exactly?" Instead of getting angry, he seemed relaxed, almost like he was enjoying himself. Probably because at this point in time, he held all the cards. Releasing his grip on me, he lowered the knife, sliding it into a black leather sheath, where it disappeared somewhere into the depths of his pocket. "You're the one who came to harass me at my place of work."

"Fuck. Just... Whatever this is, it's between me and you. Don't drag my friends into this, okay?"

"You made sure everyone was involved when you trashed our school, remember?" He stared at me, the fire burning brightly in his eyes. "You brought this on yourselves."

He was right, and I didn't have anything I could say in my defence, so I played the only card I had left. "Leave Milo alone, and I'll fight you at the bowl, okay?"

There was a shocked silence, and then a wide grin appeared on his face. "You mean it?"

"Uh, yeah." Caught off guard by his smile, I had to fight to gather my thoughts. I hadn't even meant to agree to fight him, but I couldn't go back on it now. "Yeah. I'll fight you."

And I was going to take him down.

Wipe the floor with him, right in front of everyone.

Leave his reputation in tatters.

Then, I'd finally be free of Asher Henderson.

FIVE
LEVI

Sprawling on the sofa in the media room with Milo, Katie, and a few other guys from the team, I half listened as Milo went through the list of everything that needed to be done for Fright Night. This year's celebrations were taking place the day before Halloween, a day that Milo told me was known as Devil's Night, which was celebrated in some parts of the USA. "Mayhem" was the word he'd used.

It seemed fitting for our Fright Night pranks.

My phone beeped.

One new message.

Tapping to open my app, I stared at the notification, frowning as I took in the words on the screen.

Unknown: Knock knock

There was a click, and all the power went out.

"Levi!"

I heard Milo's shout, but I was already on the move, flicking on the torch on my phone. "The switches must've tr—"

My words died in my throat at the pounding on the media room door, followed by a crash as the door was thrown open. Through the dim light coming from my phone, I saw hooded figures pour into the room, and the next thing I knew, cold jets of water were coming at me from every direction, soaking through my clothes. From the shouts, my friends were experiencing the same thing. Dropping my phone, I lunged for the closest shadow, tackling them to the floor.

The person kicked out, catching my shin, but I kept hold of them, bringing up my knee to connect with whatever body part of theirs was closest. With a soft grunt, they jerked back, struggling against me, and it hit me then.

This was our payback.

Which meant that Asher was here somewhere.

They dared to attack me in my own house?

Someone else turned their phone torch on, and the shadows became clearer. They were all hooded, but I could now see the face of my assailant.

Asher's dickhead best friend, Danny. He grinned up at me and then looked over my shoulder. "This one's yours," he said, and I didn't have time to think about what his words meant before I was being yanked up and away from him, and then a way-too-fucking-familiar voice was purring in my ear.

"Miss me?"

"You made a huge mistake," I hissed through my teeth, twisting my body down and around, breaking free of Asher's grasp.

"Nah, I really didn't. Nice place you've got here, Seven—not that I can see much of it in the dark. You might wanna sort out your little power problem. We could use some light in here."

"I hate you so fucking much." My back was against the wall, and he was right up in my face. Again.

"The feeling's mutual, believe me." He caged me in, much like I'd done to him before, except this time our faces were close together, our breaths mingling. With the little light we had, my other senses were heightened, and the sound of his breathing was loud in my ear.

"Bit of a pathetic effort at payback, isn't it?" Lowering my voice, I angled my head, the stubble on his cheek rasping against my own as our faces connected.

Asher seemed to find this amusing, for some reason, his body shaking with suppressed laughter. "Yeah, I suppose it is." One of his hands came down from the wall and gripped my chin, his fingers digging into my jaw as he yanked my head to the side. Then his mouth was at my ear. "This was fun. See you soon, Seven."

The next second, the press of his body disappeared, and then there was a loud beeping sound, and he was gone.

"What the *fuck* just happened?"

My question was called out to the room in general, but it was Milo who answered. "That wasn't water."

"Smells like cheap shit tequila," one of the other guys said. "We need some light in here."

Light. Yes. I retrieved my phone from where I'd dropped it. "I'll be back." Shining the torch in front of me, I made my way through the house to the box housing the trip switches and flicked them back on.

As soon as the power came back to life, I saw the piece

of paper taped to the wall below the box. A crumpled, lined sheet that looked like it had been torn from a notebook, it had a number seven on the front, with a heart below it. I pulled it off the wall, gritting my teeth.

> GET READY FOR THE FIGHT OF YOUR LIFE.
> PREPARE TO LOSE. ASHER

Slumping against the wall with a sigh, I traced my fingers over the indentations of his name, then balled up the paper and threw it to the floor. Turning on my heel, I went to leave, but I'd only taken two steps when I found myself spinning back around and swiping the paper from the floor. I smoothed it back out, then carefully folded the note and put it in my pocket.

Re-entering the media room, I took in the scene in front of me. My foot connected with something hard and plastic, and I glanced down to see a discarded water pistol lying on the floor. I bent down to pick it up, and as soon as I lifted it, I could smell the stench of the alcohol inside it.

"They broke into my house and squirted us with water guns filled with cheap tequila?"

Milo's gaze connected with mine, a look of disbelief on his face. "Seems so."

I was almost disappointed. We'd trashed their school gym, including their uniforms, and they chose this childish trick as payback?

"Maybe they did something else. Let's check the other rooms." Out of the corner of my eye, I saw Katie's brow raise at the poorly concealed hope in my voice.

There were six of us in total, and we spread out through

the house, checking the rooms one by one, but nothing else was amiss. I even checked the garage, knowing Asher's fascination with my car—I'd seen the admiring glances he'd given it, despite his apparent disdain—but it was still exactly where I'd left it. Once we were all back in the media room, I brought up the app for our security cameras. They were set to only come on when the house was empty, but the doorbell camera was on a sensor, set to record whenever it detected movement.

There it was. I watched as a hooded figure appeared in the camera's field of vision, getting closer. When the figure was in front of the door, he lowered his hood, revealing his messy dark hair, his brown eyes full of laughter as he lifted his middle fingers to the camera with a huge grin on his face.

Wanker.

I saved the footage, then took another sweeping glance around the media room. Tequila was everywhere. All over the walls, the floor, the furniture, and the TV.

"Are you going to say anything to your parents about this?" Carl, one of our football forwards, waved a hand around the room.

"No. That could lead to questions that we don't want to answer. I'll sort it out. Does anyone remember the name of that cleaning service we used after that party when those girls thought it was a good idea to spray champagne all over the place?"

"I have the details. Want me to book them?" Milo was already pulling out his phone. "There's an online form."

"Thanks." I dropped down to the sofa, then jumped straight back up, feeling the damp fabric beneath me. "I fucking hate that dickhead."

"So you keep saying." The corners of Milo's lips tilted up in amusement, and I shot him a glare. He smirked at me. "I think we got off lightly, all things considered. Guess they're just as pathetic off the field as they are on the field."

My fingers dug into my pocket, touching the corner of the paper inside, and I *knew*.

This wasn't over yet.

In the darkness, his body pressed against me, hot and hard. His stubble dragged across my cheek as he lowered his head.

"Levi." My name fell from his lips, and I shuddered against him, my cock lengthening at the feel of his body against mine.

I groaned, tipping my head back, pulling him closer to me. He responded by sliding his lips down my throat. Fuck, I needed to kiss him. Needed to learn how he tasted.

When he raised his head, our gazes collided, and the banked heat in his eyes set me on fire. How had I managed to resist him for so long?

I gripped the back of his head, closing the final inch of space between us. "Ten."

My eyes flew open, my heart pounding.

What the fuck? Glancing at my phone, I saw it was just past four in the morning.

My cock was hard.

I'd been dreaming about Asher, and now my fucking dick was hard?

A growl tore from my throat as I slammed my hands down on the bed in frustration. It wasn't enough for Asher to torment me in person, he had to invade my dreams, too?

And why the fuck did I have an erection?

Without permission, my hand slid under the covers and then under the band of my grey sleeping shorts. When my fingers wrapped around my cock, I groaned. I was so close to the edge already.

My mind focused on sexy, soft curves, my usual fantasy of a hot brunette woman spread out naked on my bed, ready for me. Fisting my cock, I lost myself in the fantasy, except the second I got into it, the woman disappeared, and in her place was Asher.

Fuck. There was no way I was going to get myself off while thinking about my nemesis. No. Way. Releasing my aching erection, I withdrew my hand with a frustrated breath.

Why did I let him get inside my head like this? It wasn't even the fact that I'd been dreaming about a guy—it had happened before, once or twice, and maybe occasionally my porn selections veered away from straight and into gay. But that wasn't the point. It was that it was *Asher Henderson*. That was fucked up on so many levels.

My head was a mess, my dick was hard, and now I was too worked up to fall asleep again. Reaching for my phone, I hit the web browser to take my mind off everything.

I meant to, anyway.

Instead, I opened my messages and found the single message from the unknown number that I'd received earlier, right before the lights went out. My finger was hitting the button to reply before I was even fully aware of what I was doing.

Me: You're going to regret what you did

Almost as soon as I'd placed my phone down, the message alert sounded. My heart pounding, I fumbled for my phone.

Unknown number: Couldn't sleep either?
Unknown number: I wondered when I'd hear from you
Me: How did you get my number?
Unknown number: Your social media isn't very private. Might want to look at that
Me: Fuck you
Unknown number: Did you like my love letter?

My fists clenched, my phone case digging into my skin. How could Asher Henderson antagonise me so much, even through a phone screen? I glanced over to my desk, where I'd placed the note he'd left me. I should've thrown it in the bin.

Me: Again, fuck you
Unknown number: What did you name me in your contacts? Let me guess. Something unimaginative. Ten? Or was it more flattering, like My Hero?

My hatred for this guy was growing by the second.

Me: Wrong. I didn't save your number

His reply took a long time to come, and when it did, his only response was a thumbs up.
A sting of disappointment spiked in my chest, and I immediately cursed myself. Why should I care that he sent me a dismissive thumbs up?

Before I even knew what I was doing, I was tapping out a reply and hitting Send.

Me: I saved you as LOSER if you must know

Then I did save his number to my contacts.
He responded in under a minute.

Loser: As unimaginative as I thought
Me: What did you save me as then?
Loser: Wouldn't you like to know. Why are you awake anyway?

That was a question that I was never going to answer honestly, and also, why the fuck was I lying here having a conversation with the guy I hated?

Me: This conversation is boring me and I need sleep
Loser: Dream of me kicking your ass in the bowl
Me: You wish. Dream of me knocking you out
Loser: The only time that would ever happen is in your dreams
Me: I can't wait to bring you down in front of everyone
Loser: Your seriously deluded
Me: *you're
Loser: Fuck off grammar police

He also sent me three middle-finger emojis, so I sent the same back before returning my phone to my bedside table. This conversation had gone on for way too long already.

A notification lit up my screen, and I groaned, angling my phone towards me so I could read the message.

Loser: Sweet dreams 7

I didn't sleep again that night.

SIX
ASHER

Everything was in place. Every eventuality that we could think of planned for.

The stunt we'd pulled at Levi's house—that was a distraction. A way to lull them into a false sense of security.

Now, it was Devil's Night, the day before Halloween, and time for the real payback to begin.

Nothing had been left to chance. We knew that all of Alstone High would be celebrating at the Fright Night carnival at Parton Park, and the football team would be doubly occupied with their game of pranks.

If all went as planned, we'd still be able to enjoy the Fright Night festivities. Our first job was to be seen there, and then four of us would leave to carry out the next part of the plan.

I'd already parked my car earlier that day, stashing it down one of the side streets, and at 7:00 p.m., I met my friends outside the park gates. It didn't escape my notice that Danny and Talia were holding hands, and I pushed between them, slinging my arms over their shoulders. "Nice to see my two best mates have progressed to hand-holding." They both rolled their eyes at me. "Seriously, you know I'm all for this relationship."

Talia gave me a genuine smile. "We need to find you a girl so we can double-date."

"Double date? Am I the kind of person who goes on double dates?" Keeping my arms around them, I steered them towards the back of the queue of people waiting to have their tickets scanned to get inside the park.

"I don't think you need to be a specific type of person to go on a double date, Ash." She poked me in the side. "Let me set you up with someone."

"Thanks, but no thanks." Dropping my grip on them, I fished my phone from my pocket so that my entry ticket could be scanned. I didn't bother mentioning the sad truth—the closest I'd come to any action since I'd split up with Talia for the final time was when Levi had me pressed up against the shelves in the shop, his lips touching my ear... As the image flashed through my mind, a spark of heat flared to life, and I jolted. What the fuck?

Redirecting my brain as quickly as possible, I glanced around me as we entered the park. It looked much the same as it had last year. Rides and stalls decorated with neon lights, and a massive Ferris wheel and a haunted house at either end of the fairground. Sweeping coloured lights illuminated the area, accompanied by music pounding out of surrounding speakers.

We headed away from the main fairground to the skate park, where we met up with the other guys from the football team to go through the plan for tonight. Most of them had wanted to be involved, since we all wanted payback, but we needed to keep our numbers low so there was less chance of anything going wrong. So the others would be keeping things going here in the park and doing some pranks of their own, targeting the Alstone High football team players specifically. As far as I was concerned, the more distractions, the better. "Remember—me, Danny, Talia, and Omar meet by the cars in an hour. Until then, make sure you're seen by people from Alstone High, and get photo evidence."

All in agreement, everyone split off. I left them to it for now, lowering myself to the ground next to the skate bowl, in front of the graffiti wall. Two guys were in there doing tricks, and I half watched them while I ran through everything again in my head, hoping I hadn't forgotten anything.

Out of the corner of my eye, I noticed a group of hooded figures in neon Purge-style masks making their way out of the underpass that led out of the other end of the park.

The Alstone High football team. Recycling the same idea as the previous year, exactly as we'd guessed they would. The masks had been introduced during the inaugural Fright Night, and it looked like they were here to stay.

Pulling up my own hood, I fixed my focus on the skateboarders in front of me. There was a time and a place to confront Levi, and while I was on my own and he was surrounded by all his mates was not the time.

When they'd passed me, I climbed to my feet and took a selfie with the Fright Night lights in the background, and then posted it to my social media. I still had around half an hour until I needed to meet the others by the cars, so I headed back to the fairground. Stopping by a stall across from the haunted house, I watched as the masked figures began spreading out through the crowds, accompanied by the sound of a dance tune remixed with Purge sirens blaring from the speakers.

Shaking my head, I turned away from the scene. "Can I get a bag of candy floss?" I met the gaze of the woman on the food stall, and she nodded, handing me a bag in return for the cash. Pulling open the bag, I grabbed a handful and shoved it into my mouth, sighing as the fluffy sugar melted on my tongue. What could I say? I had a bit of a sweet tooth, and this stuff was pure sugar.

Wandering across to the dodgems, I noticed Danny and Talia on the ride, sharing a car. I leaned against the side of the ride to wait for them, snapping a couple of pictures, then digging back into my candy floss.

"Candy floss?"

My head shot around to see Levi standing there, hands in his pockets. His hood was down, and his mask was pushed up on top of his head. I eyed him warily but decided that it was a good thing that he'd seen me. "Yeah, Seven. Candy floss. Great observation skills. Want some?" I held out the bag.

He automatically reached into the bag and grabbed some, then froze. Wide-eyed, his grey eyes met mine. "I—uh…"

I sighed, acting casual even though I was fucking shocked that he'd taken it. "It's okay. I can share my candy floss with my mortal enemy. And no, I haven't poisoned it, before you ask."

With a shrug, he pulled his hand out of the bag, lifting the candy floss to his lips. When his tongue darted out to swipe away the remnants of sugar, I realised too late that I'd been staring at his mouth in silence for way, way too long. His gaze was on me, and I knew that he'd noticed.

Fuck. Time to redirect. "What are you doing? Shouldn't

you be off chasing girls or doing pranks or whatever you rich pricks like to do for fun?"

His eyes narrowed. "There's plenty of time for that. What are you doing, lurking around here on your own? Did your friends finally realise what a dickhead you actually are?"

"I could ask you the same thing. While we're having this little question-and-answer session, tell me. Does your room still smell of tequila?" I watched in satisfaction as his eyes flashed with anger, and he closed the distance between us, shoving against my chest. "You really like getting close to me, don't you? Watch my candy floss—don't want it to get crushed." My mood was so high, thinking of what was going to happen later, that I couldn't stop grinning. Predictably, Levi didn't like that. With a snarl, he gripped my wrist, twisting my arm around and sending my candy floss falling to the ground.

"Why won't you just fucking leave me alone?" he ground out, as if he hadn't been the one to approach me in the first place.

"What a surprise to see the two of you together."

Levi sprung away from me at the sound of the new voice, his teeth still bared, his chest rising and falling in rapid movements. I rolled my eyes, throwing a smirking Danny my middle finger. "Don't start." Bending down, I swiped my bag of candy floss from the grass. When I straightened back up, Levi had gone.

"I'm beginning to think this obsession of yours goes both ways," Talia mused as she came down the ride steps to join me.

"Both of you, stop, for fuck's sake. We have more important things to worry about now. We need to get out of here without being seen."

"Follow me." With Danny leading the way, we slipped through the shadows, out of the park, the crowds working in our favour and concealing us from any watching eyes. We'd all pulled our hoods up too, as an extra precaution, but I didn't see any masked figures from Alstone High this close to the gates.

When we reached our cars, Omar was already waiting.

Sliding into the driver's seat, I gunned the engine, grinning across at Omar, then flicked my gaze to the rear-view mirror, where behind me, Danny had started his car, Talia in the passenger seat.

I hit the accelerator.

It was time to put our plan into action.

SEVEN
LEVI

The taste of candy floss was still on my tongue when I pushed through the crowds to rejoin Milo. I shouldn't have gone over to Asher, should've steered clear, but he drew me in like a moth to a flame. Standing there illuminated by the neon lights of the dodgems, his usual scruffy, casual self, eating candy floss without a care in the world. How he always looked so good when he made no effort with his appearance…it was just one of the many things that pissed me off about him. Before I knew it, I was standing in front of him, and we were at each other's throats again.

Or I was. He'd kept his cool, the asshole, and I'd been left with a hollow, dissatisfied feeling after our encounter.

"Okay?" Even with the mask hiding Milo's face, I could hear the concern in his voice. Flipping down my own mask, I hit the switch to turn it on, lighting everything a neon green.

"I'm fine. Just a run-in with some Highnam scum."

"Forget them." He clapped me on the shoulder. "Let's get on with the games, then we can party."

"Yeah." Something was nagging at the back of my consciousness, an unease that I couldn't place. Shrugging it off, I focused on my friends. "The entries are already coming in. We'll meet at the cove to announce the winners."

Milo gave a resigned sigh. "So you're going off on your own, then? Why do I have the feeling your prank has something to do with Highnam Academy's team captain?"

"It might not." I was telling the truth. I had a few ideas for the pranks I wanted to do, but if I could get under Asher's skin at the same time, then it would be so much more satisfying. I'd video my prank and send him a copy, of course.

"If you say so." Milo gave my shoulder a shove. "Don't do anything stupid. I'll see you at the cove, if not sooner. I'll have my phone on me if you need anything, alright?"

"Thanks. I appreciate it." I watched as he disappeared off into the crowds before making my way to the edge of the park, jogging alongside the chain-link fence until I reached the cut-through that led to the side street I'd parked my car on. It seemed that Asher had the same idea as me—to park earlier in the day to get a decent spot, as I'd seen his car purely by chance when I was heading for my own space. I'd made sure to park well away from him, and my car was more or less hidden down a tiny street wreathed in shadows, where I knew it would stay undetected.

Sliding into the driver's seat and pulling off my mask, I started up the engine and carefully backed out of the small space, then headed in the direction of Asher's car. Anticipation thrummed through my veins, and I found myself grinning as I steered with one hand and tapped my fingers on my thigh in time to the beats playing on the car stereo.

When I swung into his road, I slowed to a crawl. Unlike earlier, cars were now parked on either side of the street, leaving a narrow space to drive through. I was concentrating so hard on not scraping the sides of my car that I drove straight past Asher's Honda Civic and had to stop and reverse back down the road.

Wait. I hadn't missed it.

It wasn't there.

My fingers clenched on the steering wheel as I drove slowly to the end of the road, scanning the cars either side, checking in case I'd got his parking location wrong in my head. I knew I had the right street, because I'd noted down the road name earlier.

A memory flashed in my mind—Asher, pinning me against the wall of my media room, all hard, unyielding muscles, his hands planted on either side of my head. What was it I'd said to him? *Bit of a pathetic effort at payback, isn't it*? And he'd laughed, like he knew something I didn't.

Asher was smart, and now if I thought about it...what would I do in his position?

Make them think that payback had already been served, then strike when everyone least expected it. And the best time to do that?

Fright Night, when we were all occupied with our own games.

Fuck.

Exiting the side road, I spun the wheel, directing my McLaren away from the park. They wouldn't be stupid enough to try anything at the school, surely, so that left my house. My currently empty house, since my parents were currently somewhere in Switzerland at a convention-slash-getaway. There was no doubt in my mind that I'd be the one targeted, since Asher was constantly out to get me, and on top of that, I was the team captain.

It hadn't been that long since I'd seen him at the park, so he couldn't have had much of a head start. That thought kept me going as I broke all the speed limits getting back to my house.

When I roared into the driveway, all was quiet, with no sign of other cars. I rolled my car into the garage and entered the house, but the alarms were still set—nothing had disabled them. Still, I made a quick circuit just to make sure.

Maybe I'd been wrong, and Asher had just left the Fright Night event or moved his car somewhere else and I'd missed it.

No. Neither of those options was right. I knew it in my gut. Resetting the alarms, I headed back to my car and drove in the direction of Alstone High.

Just to make sure.

When the honey-coloured stone buildings of the school came into view, I slowed down, scanning the area ahead of me for any sign of Asher's car.

Past the side of the school grounds, there was a rutted track that was part of a public footpath, used by the Alstone High cross-country running team when they were training for races. I turned into the entrance and stopped, not willing to risk my McLaren's suspension on the bumpy surface. It was enough—I only needed to shine my headlights down the track to see what I'd been looking for. Two cars, a dark blue Ford Fiesta, and behind it, a familiar black Honda Civic Type R.

Anger burned through my body. Asher was going to pay.

Backing out of the track entrance, I turned back towards the main school building. The car park would be locked, but there was a waiting area out the front of the main pillared entrance, and I pulled into that, bringing my car to a sudden stop. After checking my surroundings to make sure I was definitely alone, I grabbed my mask and yanked it over my head. Slamming the car door behind me, I took off for the gym at a run, keeping to the shadows and avoiding the security cameras that were dotted around the area.

When I rounded the back of the main school building and saw the gym in front of me, I realised I'd left my phone in my car. Fuck. I spun around, intending to run back for it, but the sound of hushed voices stopped me in my tracks. Pressed against the stone wall, I watched as three figures appeared from around the side of the gym building. My jaw tightened. As if it wasn't insult enough that they'd broken into our school, they were wearing masks. Purge-style, neon masks. *Our* masks.

Their voices carried across the still night air, and I held my breath, listening.

A smile tugged at my lips. From what I could make out of their hushed conversation, it appeared that I'd arrived just at the right time. Apparently, their leader was still inside.

When the figures had disappeared, I skulked around the back of the gym to the fire exit, which had been propped open slightly, with a brick holding it in place. That must have been how they'd managed to get in. After removing the brick and carefully edging the door closed, I managed to manoeuvre a huge, heavy industrial-sized bin in front of the door. It took me a lot longer than I'd anticipated, alternately dragging and pushing it bit by bit, and my whole body ached by the time it was in place. The ache was worth it, though—Asher wouldn't be able to make his escape until I'd dealt with him. I made a mental note to put everything back in its original position afterwards, and then I pulled my student pass from my pocket and headed around to the front of the building.

Now, I'd make Asher Henderson pay.

EIGHT
ASHER

Danny filmed me and Omar as we systematically shredded the black-and-green AHS football uniforms, while Talia kept watch at the changing room doorway. Our faces were hidden behind Purge-style masks—a nice touch Danny had thought of. It was both a taunt and a way to hide our faces from any security so nothing could be pinned on us. Once we'd finished, Danny was going to upload the footage, and with our masks, we were betting on people thinking that we were part of the Alstone High pranks. Until they watched the footage, that was, and then the AHS football team would know exactly who had trashed their school gym.

It had been easy enough to break in, after all. We'd scoped out the grounds earlier in the week, and since we were avoiding the main school buildings where the heavier security was concentrated, all it took was a pair of wire cutters and a crowbar to get inside without alerting anyone to our presence. The fire door was alarmed, but Danny's cousin's friend's brother, or something like that, was a dodgy geezer who had sorted that particular problem out for us. For a price, but it was worth it, and the whole team had chipped in. As promised, the alarm had been disabled when we entered, and so far, all had been good.

When we were finished, I wiped my knife blade on my hoodie before stowing it away. I glanced around the room at the destruction we'd caused, knowing that the state of the gym itself was even worse, and Alstone High would be out for blood after this.

Yeah, it was still worth it.

"Come on, let's get out of here." Danny pocketed his phone, shifting on his feet. "We've been here too long already."

My gaze caught on the bank of shiny black-and-green lockers at the side of the room, now marred and dented after Omar and I had been at them with the crowbar. Chewing on my lip, I debated with myself before I came to a snap decision.

"You go on ahead. Get back to Parton Park and do whatever shit you want to do there. Give it a few hours before you upload the footage, then lay low."

"Ash," Talia cautioned, but I stopped her with a raise of my hand.

"Do it. I won't be long."

"Mate. Keep your phone on you, and if you get into anything, we'll come straight back for you." Danny clapped me on the back. "Can't say I didn't see this coming. A bit of personal revenge against Alstone's football captain, huh?"

Talia coughed into her hand, the noise sounding a lot like the word "obsessed," so I ignored her, crossing over to the changing room door and holding it open so they could get out of there. "Don't get caught on your way out. I'm right behind you."

When they'd disappeared back down the corridor that led to the main gym and fire exit, I crouched down next to the small backpack I'd brought with me. The black spray paint would be no good for defacing Levi's locker, so I guess that left the pink or purple. Grabbing one of the cans at random, I shook it as I stalked back over to the bank of lockers before directing it at the central one, the one with Levi's player position and number printed on a small sign above it.

I kept it simple, taking a leaf from Levi's book and spraying a large number ten, then adding an X underneath. As the neon pink paint dripped down the shiny black surface, I smiled, satisfied. One thing left to do, and then I could get out of there.

The lockers had fingerprint sensors, unlike the ones at our school that had combination padlocks. But they were still just as easy to break into; it just took a bit of jimmying and a lot of force. I headed back to my backpack and stashed the spray can, then rummaged in the bag until my hand closed around the small tin of WD-40.

A soft noise had me springing to my feet, dropping the tin back in the bag. I stilled, listening.

There it was again. Someone was coming.

Fuck.

I zipped my backpack as quietly as I could, wincing at how loud the sound was when I was on edge and listening out for noises. Even my breathing was loud in the thick silence.

Edging out of the changing room, I ran for the corridor and the fire exit as the soft noises drew closer. Caution was forgotten—I needed to get out of there without being caught.

The fire exit loomed closer as I sped up my pace, and I huffed out a relieved breath as I lunged for it. *Almost free*.

The air was knocked from my lungs as I rebounded off the door. Someone had shut it. I pressed down against the bar to push it open, shoving at the heavy door with all my force. There was a scraping sound, but it didn't budge.

Fuck. Fuck. *Fuck*.

"Going somewhere, Ten?"

A full-body shiver went through me at the sound of that low drawl.

I smiled. Straightening up, I slowly turned around to face the masked figure. He was leaning casually against the wall, but the tension was pouring off him in waves.

Just the way I liked him.

My pulse thrummed with anticipation, fire burning through my blood.

"Seven. My own personal stalker." Lightning fast, I struck, pinning him against the wall in my favourite position. I needed to see his face, so before he had a chance to react to my body weight, I pushed his hood back and yanked his mask off his head, throwing it to the floor.

Levi's face was a mixture of shock and outrage, his teeth bared and his silver eyes flashing dangerously. His ash-brown hair was mussed from the hood, and his chest heaved against mine as his body shook with anger.

"You fucking—" He didn't even finish the sentence before he was swiping my legs out from under me, sending me crashing to the floor. Throwing himself on top of me, he yanked my mask off, the strap snapping against the side of my face when he ripped it from my head, a hot lash that burned into my skin.

The violence in his movements was unprecedented, and my confidence that I could handle him was replaced with temporary uncertainty. Struggling beneath him, I managed to get a grip on my phone. My backpack was underneath me, the contents digging into my back painfully as he held me down, but I ignored that for the moment. As much as I didn't want to admit it, I should probably call for backup.

I never got a chance. Levi rolled off me, tearing my phone from my grip as he went, and jumped to his feet, bringing his foot down onto my phone. There was a sound of glass shattering and then a loud crunch as he stamped on it again.

"That was my fucking phone, you absolute fucking bastard!" I saw red, staggering to my feet and yanking my backpack off my shoulders. Launching myself at him, I sent him falling into the wall. He collapsed with a loud exhale of breath punching from his lungs, and I grabbed him around the throat while I widened my stance so he couldn't throw me off again. I wasn't holding back anymore.

Tightening my grip on his throat, I lowered my head to his as my fingers closed around my knife. "You're going to pay for that," I snarled. "It's time I introduced you to Ruby. Properly."

Levi's eyes widened, silver ringed with smoky grey, and he stared at me defiantly from beneath his lashes. I could feel his pulse pounding underneath my fingers, and as I began to ease the knife from its sheath, he angled his head forwards, our lips almost touching.

"*Do it.*"

Then his mouth came down on mine.

NINE
LEVI

There was a loud buzzing in my head, drowning out the voice demanding what the hell I was doing. All I could focus on was Asher's lips, soft but completely unyielding against mine. He froze, his hand stilling in the process of pulling out his knife, his fingers loosening their tight grip on my throat.

"What the *fuck!*" He eventually found his voice, scrambling back from me until his back hit the opposite wall of the corridor. Panting, he stared at me, fury raging beneath the confusion in his eyes.

I didn't have a single explanation for what I'd done.

He didn't even give me any time to think before he was lunging back at me with a growl of rage, his body slamming into me and knocking the breath from my lungs.

My arms came up to push him away, but he grabbed the back of my head with both hands and smashed his lips down on mine.

Fucking hell.

He bit at my lower lip, drawing blood, attacking my mouth while his fingers dug into the back of my skull, holding me in place. I bit back, and he hissed in pain, darting his tongue out to lick his abused lip. Taking advantage of the temporary respite, I shoved him away as hard as I could, but he took me with him, tightening his grip on my skull until my head was pounding. We hit the opposite wall again, and this time Asher was the one pinned.

"I hate you *so fucking much*." His voice was a low, savage rasp. He pulled my head to his, and our mouths met again in a fight for dominance, a clash of teeth and tongues.

"I really…fucking…hate…you, too," I ground out between attacks, biting and licking, my fingers digging into his biceps. I wasn't even aware of the moment I'd touched him, but his muscles were hard and flexing beneath my palms as I squeezed as hard as I could.

As I pushed against him, he angled his hips, and something hard pressed into my thigh. A shocked gasp tore from his throat, and I jumped back from him with dawning horror, my gaze flicking down to my jeans, then his, not that I needed the visual evidence.

My cock was *hard*.

And judging from the bulge in his jeans, and what I'd just felt against me, so was his.

Asher's face was flushed, his pupils blown, and his mouth wide open as he stood there, at a total loss for words. Blood streaked across his lips, the evidence of our brutality.

My legs shaking, I took a step back from him and then another, until I hit the welcoming solid surface of the wall behind me. Inhaling a shuddering breath, I watched Asher slide to the floor, drawing up his knees and placing his head in his hands, all the fight drained out of him.

Following his lead, I lowered myself to the floor, adjusting myself so my cock wasn't painfully digging into my zipper. I managed to stifle my groan by biting down on my lip, which sent a throbbing pain across my whole mouth. With a tentative finger, I gently examined my abused lips, bruising and stinging sensations following everywhere I touched.

He'd completely fucked my mouth up. I needed ice, otherwise I was going to have a lot of explaining to do.

In fact, what I needed was to get out of here. Now.

On autopilot, I reached into my pocket for my phone to check the time, remembering too late that I'd left it in my car. I ignored the spike of guilt that appeared from smashing Asher's phone—he deserved that, and more.

I wasn't going to hang around in here. If Asher wanted to stay and get caught by security, it was his funeral.

Climbing to my feet, my legs still shaky, I propped myself against the wall and left without looking back.

When I reached the main entrance, I dug my hand in my pocket to fish out my swipe card so I could let myself out of the building.

Except it wasn't there.

Frantically, I felt for it in my other pocket, patting down my jeans, then searching the floor. I must've dropped it somewhere. It couldn't have gone far. Retracing my steps, I headed for the main gym, since that was the first place I'd searched for Asher when I'd entered the building.

I gritted my teeth, my fists clenching as I took in the state of the gym for the second time that evening. Someone had spray-painted a huge cock across the floor—my bet was on that wanker Danny. And I was also betting he was the one who'd sprayed "AHS can suck my dick" on the wall.

All the balls that were normally kept in the equipment cupboard had been scattered all over the floor, punctured and damaged. The exercise mats had been slashed, and for some reason, there were large blow-up dolls shoved inside the basketball hoops at either end of the gym.

Pushing aside my anger, I focused on searching the floor for the card, but it soon became apparent that it wasn't there. I hadn't gone far into the gym, so I was wasting my time continuing my search. Frustrated, I scrubbed my hand across my face, wincing at the immediate throbbing pain that came from my lips.

Fuck, I *really* needed to get out of here.

I made my way back out of the gym and into the changing room. Still no sign of the little plastic card. Straddling one of the benches in front of my vandalised locker (fuck you very much, Ten), I debated what my options were if I couldn't find my card.

"Lost something?"

I raised my head to see Asher standing in the doorway, back to his usual self, no hint of the shaken look that had been on his face earlier. Instead, he eyed me with a kind of amused disdain, which immediately enraged me. How could he be so unaffected by everything that was happening?

"You—"

My words cut off as I noticed what he held in his hand. A can of Sprite, condensation beading on the sides. Ice-cold. He smirked when he saw me notice, lifting the can to his bruised lips and holding it there.

"Where did you get that?"

Lowering the can again, he tipped his thumb towards the door. "Where do you think? The vending machine."

"Oh." Cash for the vending machine...yet another thing

that wasn't currently in my pockets. In fact, they were empty except for my set of keys.

He gave a loud, overexaggerated sigh and disappeared out of the door. Closing my eyes, I placed my head in my hands.

"Here."

When I lifted my head this time, Asher was standing in front of me, holding out another can. My eyes flew to his. "You—what?"

"Yeah, I can play the hero sometimes. Just take the fucking can, will you, before I'm tempted to shake it up and open it in your face."

I needed the iciness for my lips, so I swallowed my pride and took the can from him, the tips of my fingers brushing against his as I did. We both yanked our hands back, and I concentrated hard on not looking at him instead, wasting no time and putting the can on my lips.

Ahhhh. Instant relief.

Once my lips had gone almost numb, I placed the can behind me on the bench. I could feel Asher's gaze on me, and I forced myself to meet his eyes. He was facing me, also straddling the bench, a smug grin on his face.

"You can thank me now," was the first thing he said.

"For that attempt at a kiss? No, thanks, I don't enjoy having my lips smashed into my teeth. Your technique needs serious work."

His grin was instantly wiped away. "Are you fucking insane? I was referring to the can. And that. Was not. A kiss."

"What was it, then?" I stared at him. I hadn't even meant to bring up our moment in the corridor, but the words had come out, and now the air between us was crackling with tension.

"That was punishment. A physical manifestation of my hatred for you. You kissed me first, anyway."

"To stop you stabbing me, you fucking savage!"

Asher laughed, throwing his head back, and at that moment he looked so good, all I could do was stare at him in silence, caught up by the way his throat was working and his brown eyes were dancing with amusement, framed by those thick, dark lashes.

"You really thought I'd stab you." After a while, he stopped laughing, his expression turning serious again. "I might have. I guess we'll never know."

"Well, that makes me feel so much better," I muttered.

"As for the comment about my technique..." He exhaled slowly, sliding forwards on the bench so our knees were touching. His fists clenched and unclenched, his brows pulling together.

The atmosphere between us grew heavy, the tension thick in the air.

Our eyes met and held, and I couldn't fucking breathe.

Angling his head forwards, he stopped with a millimetre of distance between us, then slowly, with the barest pressure, he brushed his lips over mine. A gasp escaped me at the first touch of his mouth, but I recovered, returning the brush of his lips with my own. His hand came up to curl around the back of my neck, and I found myself moving even closer, opening my mouth to him.

He didn't deepen the kiss like I expected. Instead, he licked across my lips in languid movements, soothing the places he'd hurt me. When he pulled back, removing his hand from my neck, I chased his mouth, taking hold of his jaw and feeling the rasp of stubble beneath my fingers as I leaned forwards, carefully licking over his lips until I'd covered every inch. When I'd finished, I sat back, lowering my hands to my thighs, my fingers clenching at the denim of my jeans. My hands were shaking, and my cock was half-hard, and I was sure that I wasn't the only one affected.

"That still wasn't a proper kiss." My voice came out raspy, and I cleared my throat.

His mouth turned up at the corners. "Too painful. You'll have to imagine my superior technique." There was no taunting in his tone for once; instead, there was a hoarseness that matched mine.

I shot back a half-hearted "You wish," unsure of how to act around him when we weren't at each other's throats. It seemed Asher felt the same, because he swung himself off the bench and into a standing position, turning away from me.

"Coming?" He glanced back when he reached the door.

"Where?" I climbed to my feet, stretching.

Without answering, he started walking, so I followed him for lack of any options, keeping my gaze trained on the floor in case I spotted my card. He headed into the corridor that led to the fire exit, retrieving his bag, broken phone, and his mask. I'd snapped the strap, but he managed to fix it back on, and then he pulled his hood over his head. Swiping my own mask from the floor, I followed suit.

When he started back down the corridor the way we'd come, I spoke up. "Where are we going?"

"Out," he said shortly, increasing his pace, not stopping until we reached the front entrance.

"We can't get out this way. I lost my—"

He lifted his hand, a small, rectangular piece of plastic held between his fingers. "Card?"

Angrily yanking it from his grip, I swiped it through

the scanner and wasted no time getting out of the doors. "Where did you find that?"

"On the floor."

"How long have you had it?"

"I don't know. Some asshole broke my phone, so I don't even know what time it is."

"You deserved it."

Shaking his head, he turned towards the field that led to the track. "Sometimes I forget how much of an entitled dick you are, but you always remind me. Just because I can afford a couple of cans from the vending machine doesn't mean I'm made of money, rich boy. We can't all just snap our fingers and get a replacement whenever we want." With that parting shot, he jogged away, quickly swallowed up by the darkness.

Guilt burned through me, chased by anger. He was right, but if he hadn't been vandalising the school in the first place, none of this would have happened.

I ignored the nagging voice inside me that reminded me that Alstone High had started it first, trashing their gym.

Later that night, alone in my bed, I also tried to ignore my mind playing vivid, detailed flashbacks of the press of Asher's body against mine, his lips and tongue touching my skin, his hand around my neck...

We'd crossed a line that should never have been crossed.

We were enemies. We loathed each other with a hatred that was like a living thing, feeding off our animosity.

There would be a price to pay. I was sure of it.

TEN
ASHER

Our plan had worked out even better than we'd hoped for. Thanks to my smashed phone, I hadn't been able to get hold of any of my friends, but I'd headed straight back to Fright Night and managed to get lucky, finding Omar with a couple of the other guys from the football team. We'd made it back to Talia's place along with the rest of the team and some of their girlfriends—since she was the only one who had enough space to squeeze the entire football team in without us sitting on top of each other. Just. We still ended up on arms of chairs, on any available bit of floor space, on the coffee table...in short, we were crammed in. But we were all there.

Danny had connected his phone to the TV, and we'd viewed the footage. Ours was met with cheers and whistles, everyone talking over each other. Talia brought out some sours so we could do celebratory shots, and the volume increased even further. Euphoric. That was how everyone had been feeling. As well as our prank, the rest of the football team had been busy, and we scrolled through over an hour of footage and photos, seamlessly interspersed with the Alstone High pranks so that it would be impossible to guess who was behind them.

Except for our little stunt at Alstone High's gym. That footage quite clearly belonged to Highnam Academy.

"Nice camerawork, mate." I clapped Danny on the shoulders, and he gave me a pleased smile. I knew how much he wanted to get into the film industry. Yeah, this was only phone footage, and it would never make it onto his university application since what we'd done was illegal, but even with all that, there was no denying his skill.

That had been last night. Today was Sunday, actual Halloween, and I was due at work for the late shift. At least no one would be home when the trick-or-treaters turned up. My mum hated it if she was home, turning all the lights out and hiding behind the curtains, pretending like she wasn't in. Lucky for her, she was also going to be at work.

I still had a bit of a hangover when my shift started. Bloody Talia and her shots. They were lethal. The end of the evening had faded into a drunken haze.

But I could remember the part of the evening before her house all too well.

That was why I was currently blasting music through my earphones in an attempt to drown out the noise inside my own head.

The shop was busy—mostly in the aisle that contained all the sweets, with people buying last-second supplies for trick-or-treating. Consequently, I was busy, keeping that aisle replenished, along with my usual restocking. Things didn't slow down until around 9:00 p.m., when most of the kids were finally in bed.

Selina got up from her position behind the till when the shop was finally empty. "Swap for a bit? I feel like rigor mortis is setting in, the amount of time I've been frozen in this position."

I nodded, grabbing the bottle of water I'd been drinking to keep my headache at bay. "Yeah, alright. I was just about to start cleaning the fridges."

She shot me a glare, because that was her least favourite job, and I gave her an innocent smile. Because I'd cleaned them on my last four shifts, she just sighed and headed out the back to grab the cleaning supplies, while I headed around the counter to take a seat in front of the till. Normally I'd occupy myself with games on my phone while it was quiet, but as of today, my phone was Danny's brother's backup phone, a huge, heavy brick that probably belonged in a museum. It didn't play any games, other than Snake, which I'd been told was retro.

At least I could listen to music on it, although my Bluetooth headphones didn't work. I'd had to borrow earphones, too. Not for the first time, anger towards Levi ignited in my veins, but I pushed that aside, because thinking about Levi in any capacity led to memories that I wanted to scrub from my mind. What the fuck had possessed me to do what I did?

I increased the volume of my headphones, blasting the music at a level that would most likely damage my eardrums, but that was what I needed at this point in time.

Someone slammed a bar of chocolate down on the counter, and I jerked out of the stupor I'd fallen into, my head flying up as I hit the button to pause the music so I could serve the customer. From behind them, I noticed Selina shaking her head at me. *Swap back*, she mouthed, and I gave her a quick nod, putting the purchase through the till, and then when the customer had left, we switched places. She'd cleaned the fridges, but the shelves still needed refilling before we closed for the night, so I headed into the stockroom. The battery on the piece-of-shit phone had died, so I wrapped the earphones wire around it and shoved it in my pocket. At least there was only half an hour until my shift ended. Half an hour to avoid all thoughts of certain people and situations that I really didn't want to think about.

When I was breaking open a cardboard box, using my handy knife to slice through the tape, I heard the stockroom door open. My senses were on high alert, and without even turning around, I knew who it was. I'd known retribution was coming, but I hadn't expected it so soon.

I slowly straightened up.

"I'd rate your stalking skills four out of ten. You've got to work on the sneaking up on people thing."

Hot breath hit my ear, and a hard body bumped up against my back. "Shut up."

"Don't like criticism? Okay, five out of ten, since I'm feeling generous."

"Shut. Up." Levi used his body weight to propel me forwards, and taken by surprise, I stumbled. I would've probably fallen, except he grabbed me around the waist. "Fuck. You're so—" He gave an angry growl. "I hate you."

"So you keep saying. It's mutual, in case you forgot."

Why the fuck was his arm around my waist, holding me against his body, and why hadn't I broken out of his hold?

Just as I questioned myself, he released me and pushed at my back, hard. This time I did fall forwards, crashing into the rack in front of me, and I only just managed to throw out my hands in time to brace myself and stop me face-planting the metal shelves.

I really, really wanted to retaliate, to push at him until he snapped, but I wasn't going to risk my job. Instead, I took several calming breaths before slowly turning to face him. "What do you want? Payback?"

Levi took a step closer, his jaw clenched so tight it had to be giving him a headache. "Do you realise just how many people you've pissed off by doing what you did? The fucking *audacity* of uploading it to our private server. And using our masks?"

"You don't own the design," I pointed out, which just made him even angrier. He took a deep, enraged breath, and I knew he was going to snap.

Worry for my job overrode everything, and my mind gave me only one option. The one thing that I shouldn't ever do again, but it was the only thing that I knew would stop him in his tracks.

I closed the space between us and kissed him forcefully.

There was a second when time seemed to stop, and then—

He kissed me back.

His tongue stroked over mine as I backed him into a shelving rack, gripping onto the cool metal shelf either side of his shoulders. I kissed him harder, my tongue licking into his mouth, sparks of sensation racing all over my body. When his teeth connected with my lip, I steeled myself for the burst of pain, but instead of pain, I got pleasure when he lightly bit down, his tongue immediately licking over the sting.

"Fuck," I panted, pulling back. My cock was raging, and I couldn't remember ever getting hard this quickly before.

My brain couldn't fucking deal with any of it—the fact he was a man, he was my mortal enemy, we'd just been at each other's throats right before we kissed. *Nothing* about this was normal for me.

We stared at each other, breathing hard, my shock reflected in Levi's darkened eyes. When his tongue darted out to swipe across his lip, my dick fucking jumped, and I stumbled backwards, the need to get away from him overriding my other panicked thoughts.

To my relief, he was just as desperate to get away from me as I was from him. "I need to leave," he ground out, pushing me aside and stalking out of the stockroom. The door slammed loudly behind him.

I let him go, angrily scrubbing my hand over my face as I attempted to make sense of what had just happened.

But there was no way I could make any sense of it.

By the time my shift was over and I was walking home, my head was pounding and my brain hurt from thinking. Selina had even commented on how distracted I was, although miraculously, she hadn't seen Levi going in or out of the stockroom. In the end, the only conclusion I could come to was that our rivalry had built up so much that it had become something too big to control. It needed an outlet, and that was the only reason that this weird shit was happening between us. Kissing him? I wasn't even interested in men, let alone a rich asshole who made my life hell. Yeah. The rivalry was the only explanation.

What we needed was a proper fight. In the bowl, surrounded by crowds. I'd give Levi the beating of his life, and then I'd be free of him. Since he'd already agreed to fight me, and I knew our Fright Night stunt was fresh in everyone's minds, it was best to do it as soon as possible.

Stopping outside my front door, I fished out my keys, almost tripping over the small box that had been left beneath the doorstep. Great. Bloody delivery drivers—didn't they realise that everything that got left outside was liable to be stolen almost as soon as it had been left?

Picking up the box, I let myself into the darkened house, closing the door quietly behind me so I didn't wake my mum. My stomach rumbled, reminding me that I hadn't eaten since the sandwich I'd had at lunch, so I headed into the kitchen, flipping on the light and then placing the box on the table. After hunting through the cupboards, I grabbed a pack of chicken noodles and filled the kettle.

While I waited for it to boil, I glanced over at the box, realising that it only had my name on it, not my address. Not a delivery driver, then. Suspicious, I examined the outside, then shook it experimentally. Nothing rattled inside, so I made the decision to open it.

When I lifted the lid, I saw another box inside. There was a piece of paper on top, and I unfolded it, my heart pounding harder as I read the words written there.

> IT'S NOT NEW, AND I DIDN'T PAY MONEY FOR IT.
> IF YOU DON'T WANT IT, DONATE IT OR GET RID
> OF IT. I DON'T CARE.
> NOW WE'RE EVEN.
>   LEVI

Underneath the paper, within the box, was a phone.

My whole body stiffened. This had to be a trick, surely.

I ate my noodles slowly, debating what to do. If, on the off chance, it wasn't a trick, what would me accepting the phone signify? Would Levi expect something in return?

Yeah, the note said we were even, but I couldn't see why he'd just give me a phone, even though he'd been the one to break mine. I knew I wouldn't give him one, not only for the fact that I wouldn't be able to afford to replace his custom top-of-the-range model.

In the end, I charged up my borrowed brick phone and called Talia.

She answered after a few rings. "Hi. What's up?"

"I have a hypothetical question for you." Leaning back in the kitchen chair, I traced my finger over the smooth black metal curves of the phone Levi had sent me. There were a few surface scratches, but it looked to be in good condition other than that.

"Go on..."

"Say you broke something belonging to someone else. Would you replace it, even if you really disliked that person?"

A sigh came through the speaker. "Is this about the fact that Levi broke your phone? What's happened now?" I'd told her and Danny what had gone down in the gym after they'd gone. I might have omitted a few details...okay, most of the details, but they knew he'd broken my phone.

"He sent me a replacement with a note."

"He did? What did the note say?" The intrigue in her voice was clear. I read the note out to her and waited for her verdict. It wasn't long in coming. "If it was me...to answer your original, not-at-all-hypothetical question, yes, I would replace whatever I broke if I could. As for the fact that Levi was the one to give you the phone, it sounds to me like he wouldn't take it back from you even if you refused to accept it. So I think you should swallow your pride and keep it."

"But that means I have to thank him," I groaned,

slumping back in my chair.

"I'm sure you can manage."

"Are you rolling your eyes at me?"

She laughed. "Maybe. Seriously, though, just keep it, Ash. Thank him and move on."

Thank him and move on.

It sounded simple enough.

Too bad it wasn't.

ELEVEN
LEVI

I lowered my game controller and climbed to my feet, heading over to the drinks fridge to grab a can of Coke. Standing in front of the fridge, I massaged my temples, unsuccessfully attempting to stave off the headache that was threatening. Today had been a nightmare from the beginning. As soon as I'd shown up at school, people were jumping on me, asking what our plan for revenge was, throwing out suggestions, desperate for payback. The problem was we fucked with Highnam Academy, they fucked back harder. The way I saw it, we'd sealed our fate the minute we'd stepped onto the football pitch with them, back in the preseason match, and now the consequences of our actions had spun out of control, with no end in sight.

I'd just placed my can down on the low side table when someone cleared their throat behind me.

I turned around slowly, knowing who I'd see there, just as he'd been aware of my presence in the shop last night.

As my eyes met Asher's, he held up his hands, his gaze

wary. "I'm not here to fight. I came to say one thing, and then I'm leaving." Reaching into his pocket, he pulled out the phone that I'd left outside his house. "Thanks."

He muttered the word, dropping his gaze as he shoved the phone back into his pocket, and then turned on his heel to leave.

"Wait."

"What?" His back still to me, he paused with his hand on the door.

"Why thank me in person? And how did you get into my house?"

A dark chuckle came from him, and he turned to face me. He gave a casual shrug, his lips tilting up at the corners. "You should know by now that I like to fuck with your head, Seven."

His gaze slid past me to the TV. Before I had a chance to react to his extremely irritating presence in my house, he'd crossed the room and was picking up my discarded game controller.

"What are you doing?"

He was right next to me now, his gaze fixated on the huge screen. "Huh?" Seemingly remembering where he was, he glanced over at me with a sudden grin that took me aback. "Want to lose to me again?"

"I never lost to you in the first place." What was actually going on here? Somehow, I found myself sitting down and grabbing an extra controller. Asher threw himself down at the other end of the sofa, navigating through the game screens like he had every right to be all up in my shit.

"I put our names down on the fight rota for Sunday," he announced casually, as if it was no big deal.

"What? You didn't even ask me first?" I exhaled harshly,

my fingers clenching on my controller.

"You agreed to fight me, and I think we need to work off some tension, don't you?"

I glanced over at him. He was staring at the screen, worrying his bottom lip with his teeth, and I took a second to study the defined lines of his jaw and cheekbones, his face slightly flushed in the dim lighting of the media room.

Tearing my gaze away from him, I tapped my controller to select my character. "Uh." I cleared my throat. "Yeah. Everyone wants blood."

We were silent while the fight screen loaded, and then he blew out a frustrated breath. "Maybe when I kick your ass, everyone will finally be happy."

"I doubt it." Mashing buttons, I struck his character with a jump-kick combo, knocking him back. "You won't win, anyway."

He retaliated with a lashing whip attack, striking my character down. "That's what you think. I never lose."

"That's not true." I hit a combination that sent lightning flying out of my character's palms. His character fell to the floor, and it was game over.

"I might have temporary setbacks, but don't underestimate me, Seven. I never lose. Not in the long run."

When I glanced over at him again, his jaw was set, his eyes hard. He was right. I shouldn't underestimate him.

"What am I fucking doing?" he muttered to himself, then abruptly stood.

"Don't be a bad loser, Ten. Play again." I didn't even know why I was trying to persuade him to stay. On the list of people I wanted to spend time with, he was right at the bottom, underneath several serial killers.

He stood there for a minute, his gaze bouncing around

the room, then threw himself back down, picking up the controller. I took his silence as assent and cued up a new game.

That game turned into another, and another. By the time we'd finished our sixth game, we were both even.

"Last game to decide the winner." At this point, Asher was sprawled out on my sofa like he hung out here all the time, his thigh brushing against mine every time he shifted in his seat. "Want to make a bet?"

"What kind of bet?" I eyed him cautiously. Even though we'd been sitting here like we were friends or something, I hadn't forgotten that we were as far from friends as it was possible to get.

"If I win…" He turned to face me, a grin curving over his lips. "I get to drive your car."

"No fucking way," I said immediately, then followed it up with, "I *knew* you liked my car."

"Whatever." His brown eyes met mine, sparking with a challenge. "Are you gonna accept, or are you too scared?"

"What do I get if—no, *when* I win?"

He shrugged. "What do you want? Pick something."

What could I pick that would cause maximum enjoyment for me and maximum annoyance for him? I chewed on my lip, deep in thought.

"You know what?" He knocked my knee with his. "You don't even need to pick anything. I'm going to win."

I smiled at his cocky attitude. Taking him down would be so satisfying. "Prepare to lose."

To begin with, it seemed like it would be a close fight. What Asher didn't realise was that I was lulling him into a false sense of security. When he grew complacent, I struck. Using every trick I knew, I systematically destroyed his character, piece by piece.

When the Game Over screen appeared, he threw the controller down, and I steeled myself for his anger. Anticipated it, even. Except he surprised me with a heavy sigh, turning to face me with a resigned expression on his face.

"Alright, you won, so I guess that means you get to collect on the bet. What do you want?"

My controller slipped out of my hand, falling to the floor, but neither of us paid it any attention as he held my gaze.

The silence was so thick he could've cut it with his knife.

"I want—" Stopping myself, I shook my head to rid it of the thought that had come out of nowhere. My gaze dropped to his mouth, against my will.

Asher swallowed hard, his eyes darkening. "Tell me."

"I want..." I shifted my body towards him, my heart hammering against my ribs. What was I doing?

The words wouldn't come, but it didn't matter. As soon as I leaned forwards, his mouth was on mine.

This time when we kissed, I didn't hold back.

Neither did he.

He wasted no time in pushing me down onto the sofa so I was on my back, his body a solid weight against mine that felt so fucking good. My dick was responding to him far too quickly for my liking, and I tried to shift my hips away from him to hide how he was affecting me. But he didn't let me go, kissing me harder and pressing his own erection against my leg.

His erection. I had another cock against me for the first time, and based on the response of my dick and the way my heart rate was going through the roof, I liked it. A lot. When he pulled back to take a breath before taking my mouth again, my gaze went between us, my breath catching in my throat at the sight. The faded grey tracksuit bottoms he was wearing were doing nothing to conceal how hard he was. And how big. Maybe even bigger than me. My dick was rock solid by this point, straining against the cotton of the shorts I'd worn for lounging around in.

My groan was swallowed by his kiss as his lips came down on mine again.

"What the fuck are we doing?" He ripped his mouth away from mine, staring down at me as I sucked in a shaky breath. His pupils were so wide, the soft brown of his irises barely visible, and his lips were wet and swollen from our kisses.

"Fuck knows." My hand slid around the back of his neck, pulling his head back down to me. "I still hate you."

"Still mutual," he murmured against my lips before I ended the conversation with another kiss. I widened my legs, and he settled between them.

Fucking hell.

His cock slid against mine, and I gasped into his mouth. He rolled his hips tentatively, a groan tearing from his lips as I arched up into him.

"Fuck. This is…fuck," he panted.

"Yeah. Don't stop."

Asher obliged by kissing me again, licking into my mouth as he ground his cock against mine. One of my hands gripped the back of his head, his hair soft under my fingertips, and the other curled around his back, feeling his muscles flex under my touch.

"I'm not gay," I gasped as he moved to mouth at my jaw while his hips continued to grind down, a rhythm that had my eyes rolling back in my head.

"Me neither." His teeth scraped across my skin, followed by his tongue. "Still hate you."

"Still hate you." My short nails scraped down his scalp as I matched his rhythm.

"This feels so fucking good." He buried his face in my neck, biting at my throat in a way that made my dick throb. The slide of his cock against mine was already tipping me over the edge, and if we didn't stop, I was going to embarrass myself by coming in my shorts.

I moved my hand away from the back of his head and lowered it to grip his ass. He jerked against me, then ground into me even harder, his panted breaths hot on my neck.

Everything about him was hot. And hard.

I never wanted it to end.

Too soon, my balls tightened, and it was game over for me. His hips stuttered when I lost my rhythm, my head thrown back and my grip on his ass loosening as my dick pulsed, hot cum soaking through the fabric of my shorts.

His teeth clamped down on my skin, and then he was coming, too, stifling his groans in my throat.

Fucking hell.

Without me giving it any conscious thought, my hand stroked up his back and into his hair, both of us struggling to regulate our breaths.

Then everything crashed into my mind in one go, my brain blaring a red alert so loud that my body instantly reacted, shoving him away from me. He lost his balance, falling to the floor, barely missing the low table in front of the sofa.

"Wh—"

His shout of rage didn't even make it past his lips.

There was a sound of heavy footsteps outside, and he clamped his mouth shut as we shared a panicked glance.

Someone was coming.

TWELVE
ASHER

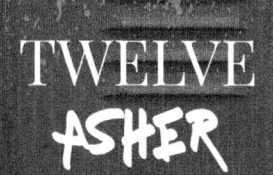

"Get up!" Levi shoved at my shoulder urgently.

"What am I supposed to do?" I didn't want to get caught here, but it wasn't like there was anywhere to hide.

"There." He pointed over my shoulder. "Quick."

I moved in the direction he'd indicated without even looking until I was standing in front of the wooden cabinet at the side of the room. A huge cabinet, yeah, but there was no way I'd fit in there comfortably. Shaking my head, I went to move away, but he stopped me with a hand to my chest.

"*Please*. I owe you."

Levi owing me? I couldn't pass that up, no matter how uncomfortable I was. "Fine." I crouched down, contorting my body to fit inside. "You owe me so fucking much for this," I hissed as he shut the door on me.

After that, all I could hear was muffled voices. I couldn't even attempt to move, and my leg was cramping up. Why the fuck was I hiding? Because I was in enemy territory, I guessed.

But if I had to hide in here for much longer, I couldn't be held responsible for the consequences of my actions.

Lucky for both of us, the voices died away, and the cupboard swung open before I could burst out of there.

"Milo," Levi said breathlessly as I climbed out. "I had to make up a story about feeling ill. Not sure he bought it."

I looked him up and down, taking in his flushed cheeks and swollen lips and the obvious damp patch on his navy shorts. Smirking, I leaned against the wall, folding my arms across my chest. "He might not have bought it, but I bet he knew you were getting up to something in here. Now, are you gonna let me borrow something to wear? I'm not driving home like this."

"No."

"You are. And while you're getting me some clothes, I'm going to think about how you can repay me for making me hide just now."

He glared at me. "Fuck, you're annoying."

I shrugged. It was probably true. But I loved winding him up. He looked so fucking hot when he was all angry—no, wait. I didn't think he was hot.

Maybe I did.

"Come on, then," he huffed, thankfully interrupting my spiralling thoughts. "I'm sure I have some old clothes I was going to donate. You can have them instead."

"Fuck you." I gave him the finger. "You can give me your nicest joggers, thanks."

"Nope."

I followed him through his massive house, up the stairs and down a long corridor, where he pushed open a door, revealing a huge bedroom decorated in deep blue tones.

"My enemy's lair, at last." Giving him an evil grin, I crossed to his big bed and flung myself onto it. Soft, yet firm, it was the most comfortable bed I'd ever lain on. "Fuck, this bed is amazing," I groaned, stretching out across the navy duvet.

Levi made a choked noise in his throat, staring at me with wide eyes, and then before I knew it, he was throwing himself onto the bed, pinning me down with his full body weight.

"Who are you to just come into my room and help yourself to my bed?" He was angry, but beneath the anger, lust was burning.

It was the same for me.

I got him into a hold and flipped us so I was on top, pinning him down. "Mmm. Much better." Lowering my head, I nipped at his jaw. "What would your friends say if they could see you now, consorting with the enemy?"

Twisting, he spun us over again. The soft duvet cradled my back as his hard body pressed into my front. "They'd say I was insane. Certifiable." His lips came down on mine in a quick, hard kiss before he pushed himself up and off me. His voice grew quiet. "Insanity is the only explanation for this."

"Yeah." I watched as he moved off the bed and over to his drawers.

He pulled out a bundle of fabric and threw it at me, then pointed towards the door next to the drawers. "Bathroom's through there." Then he disappeared out of the room, a pair of shorts in his hand.

I was surprised that he'd left me to my own devices, in his bedroom of all places. Of course I was going to take advantage, but first of all, I needed to clean up. Helping myself to his shower, I quickly washed myself, then pulled on the tracksuit bottoms he'd given me. Soft, black, some designer brand, they hugged me in a way that made my ass and dick look great, if I did say so myself. Glancing at myself in the mirror, I ran a hand through my hair and decided it was past time that I explored his inner sanctum. The bathroom itself threw up no clues—oh, except the medicine cabinet, which was full of hair products. I untwisted the lid on one of the pots, giving it an experimental sniff.

"You really should introduce your hair to some of that."

Almost dropping the pot at the sound of Levi's voice, I spun around to see him paused in the doorway, watching me, a fresh pair of shorts, this time in grey, riding low on his hips.

My gaze tracked over the hard planes of his body and up to his face, his soft lips parted and his blond-tipped lashes lowered as he completed his own thorough inspection of my body.

I swallowed hard. "My hair's fine," I said hoarsely.

He took a step closer, then another until he was right in front of me. "It's a fucking travesty, is what it is. Have you even heard of a brush?" Planting one hand on the sink beside me, he slid the other hand into my hair. "Such a mess."

The pot I'd been holding was dropped into the sink as I gave in to the inevitable, sucking Levi's bottom lip between mine, then kissing him. My cock was swelling, reacting to his proximity as he kissed me back, slowly and thoroughly, until I lost both my breath and my mind.

"What's happening?" Releasing me, he licked his lips as he stared at me with confusion written all over his face. "Why is this happening?"

"I don't know." How could I give him an answer? "I don't

know why. I've never even looked at another guy. Not even once. And *you*? I can't stand the sight of you, so why are you, of all people, fucking with my head like this?" I shook my head. "*None* of it makes any fucking sense."

"I can't stand the sight of you, either." A soft sigh fell from his lips, and he lowered his gaze, his cheeks flushing as he continued, mumbling the words in a low voice like he didn't really want me to hear them. "I've watched some gay porn, and I…I liked it. I've never met another guy in real life that's…uh…had this effect on me, though." His voice grew louder again. "But I don't like you. I hate you."

"I know. Same." We needed to get off this topic, and fast. Both of us were way too fucked up in the heads to deal with this right now.

I slid away from him, creating some much-needed distance between us. "What are the odds of you hanging around in here while I snoop in your bedroom?"

Levi snorted, a look of relief crossing his face at the change of subject. "Zero."

"Shame. Oh, well. I guess we'd better go for a drive, then."

"What?" Tilting his head, he eyed me with suspicion.

I flashed him a grin. "You owe me for making me hide in that cabinet, so I decided that you're going to let me drive your car."

He shook his head, moving in the direction of the doorway. "Never going to happen."

Swiping my T-shirt and hoodie from the floor, I pulled them on and then followed him back into his bedroom. "I'm a great driver. I won't hurt your precious car."

"I don't believe it."

"It's true. Ask anyone that knows me. I can handle any

car, even yours. My driving skills are legendary. In fact, if we were in a race, I could beat you, even with your car's advantage." *Stop talking right now.*

From his position, seated on the edge of his bed, he looked up at me, brows raised. "I doubt that. You honestly think you could beat my McLaren in your Honda Civic?"

"Easily." It was a lie, and we both knew it. What was wrong with me? I needed to keep my mouth shut.

"Fine." He stood. "We'll race, my car against yours. If you win, you can drive my car. If you lose, your car is mine."

"Huh? How is that fair?" My brows pulled together as I stared at him.

"I thought you said you could easily beat me." The asshole smirked at me. He'd backed me into a corner, and he knew that there was no way I could really win in a race against his car.

"No deal. Sorry."

"Too scared?"

I moved towards the door. Time to make my escape before he goaded me into a decision that I really shouldn't be making.

"See you on Sunday, Seven. Good luck. You're going to need it."

THIRTEEN
ASHER

How was it only Wednesday? This week needed to be over. All anyone at school was talking about was fucking Alstone High and its football captain, who was the one person I'd been trying to get out of my head. But there was no escape from Levi Woodford. If he wasn't being talked about, he was taking up uninvited space in my brain. What we'd done on Monday…he'd said insanity was the only explanation, and that was one thing we could both completely agree on. There was no rational explanation for what had gone down between us since Fright Night.

Lying back on my bed, I scrubbed my hand across my face. Fuck. Maybe I was going about this the wrong way. Maybe what I needed to do was to antagonise him—to remind both him and my brain that he was my enemy.

Mind made up, I reached for my phone.

Me: You're going down on Sunday

Levi's reply came through less than a minute later.

Seven: You wish
Me: I don't need to wish. I know
Seven: How can you irritate me so much even through a phone screen?

A smile tugged at my lips.

Me: One of my many skills
Seven: One of your few skills, you mean
Me: I didn't hear you complaining about my skills on Monday

Fuck, *no*. This was not what I was supposed to be doing. I was supposed to be reminding us both that we were enemies. Before he had a chance to reply, I sent another text.

Me: Still hate you
Seven: OK there's one or two things max that you're good at. But you're still going to lose
Seven: Still hate you too BTW

That was better.

Me: I have many skills that you've never even seen. Maybe if your good I'll show you some
Seven: *you're
Seven: What kind of skills?

For fuck's sake. Now my mind was going to a place it had no business going to.

Me: FIGHTING SKILLS
Me: Also stop correcting my fucking grammar
Seven: No need to shout

This wasn't working. Texts could be misunderstood. Maybe we needed to speak. Yeah, that would be better. I hit the Call button, and two rings later, Levi answered.

"Hello?" he said, like he didn't know it was me.

"Seven. When I win our fight, are you gonna let me drive your car?"

His irritated huff of breath was loud in my ear. "Is there a reason you interrupted my evening, other than to harass me with your delusions?"

"Interrupted? Why, what were you doing? Let me guess…you were sitting around counting all your money."

"What the fuck?" He tried to stifle his snort of laughter, but I heard it. "Actually, no. I was calculating the gains of my investment portfolio."

"Such a rich boy." For some reason, I was smiling. "I should've known."

"Really, though, why are you interrupting my evening? I was in the middle of watching the football highlights."

I glanced at my TV, which was also showing the football highlights, and reached for the remote, flicking it to a different channel. Then I flicked it back. What was it about Levi that made me act so fucking irrationally? And how could I answer his question? Calling him had seemed like a good idea at the time, but now it made no sense to me.

"Because I know you love the sound of my voice."

"Or maybe you love the sound of mine, since you were the one that phoned me," he suggested, and I just *knew* he was smirking down the phone. Time for another subject change.

"How's your school gym looking now?"

An angry growl came through the speaker. "No thanks to you, the team had to pay for it. It was that, or get the police involved, and then the papers probably would've found out about it."

"Yeah, and we all know that Alstone High has a reputation to uphold. How much other shit has been hidden? Do you just throw money at your problems to make them go away?"

There was silence, then he said, "Usually, yeah."

I laughed, hearing the amusement in his tone. "Total shocker, Seven."

"Who's that girl that you're always hanging around with?"

I blinked, caught off guard by his sudden subject change. When he cleared his throat, I realised that I'd taken too long to reply. "Talia?"

"Yeah."

"Why?"

"Just asking. You seem close."

My brows pulled together as I tugged my lip between my teeth. Why was Levi asking me about Talia?

"Why, are you jealous?"

"No," he said, far too quickly, and I smiled.

"If you say so."

"I'm not jealous," he bit out.

Such a liar. "She's one of my best mates, if you really wanna know. We had a thing, on and off, a while ago, but that's in the past. She's with Danny now."

"Do you still like her?" The words sounded like they'd been dragged out of him, like he really didn't want to ask them but couldn't help himself.

"Not in that way, no. We're friends. That's it." For some reason, I kept talking, when I really should've shut my mouth. "We've been over for a long time, and you're the only person I've done anything with since then."

There was a sharp intake of breath in my ear, and then Levi spoke. "What? You—but you're... How is that even possible? Have you seen yourself?"

"Are you telling me you think I'm hot?" I smirked into the phone.

"Fuck off. I'm saying, the way you look, you must have opportunities."

"Yeah, well, I haven't been interested. What about you? The way you look, you must have opportunities." I threw his words back at him.

"I've had a few girlfriends. Nothing serious. I haven't even kissed anyone since the summer. Probably around the time of our first football match, come to think of it."

"Too preoccupied with enacting your revenge after our team beat yours?" I suggested, knowing it would rile him up. When his frustrated huff of breath came through the speaker, I smiled, but my smile died away when he finally spoke again.

"Too preoccupied with *you*, Ten." His voice had gone all husky and low, and my dick reacted instantly.

"Why do you fuck with my head like this?" I pressed the heel of my hand down onto my dick in a failed attempt at willing it into submission.

"I'm not doing it on purpose. Why do you fuck with mine?"

"I don't know." How could I explain what I didn't even understand myself?

He sighed. "I'm going now. See you Sunday."

"Leave me here with a hard-on, thanks."

Fuck. Fuckfuckfuck. I did *not* mean to say that.

A choked noise came through the phone. "*Ten*. You got hard from talking to me?"

I remained silent. I'd already said too much. My hand snaked down into my underwear, and I gripped my cock.

"I'm hard too." His voice was breathless.

Palming my erection, I bit down on my lip to stifle a groan. This couldn't be happening. Not with him on the other end of the phone. The whole point of this had been to try and get him out of my head.

"I'm, uh. We should get off the phone."

"Yeah," he agreed.

Before either of us could say or do anything else incriminating, I ended the call, throwing my phone across the bed.

Then I gave in to the inevitable.

And when I came, Levi's face was on my mind and his name was on my lips.

FOURTEEN
LEVI

It was Friday. Still two days until my fight with Asher. Word about our upcoming clash had spread, and as I ascended the stone steps of Alstone High, I realised just how much things had spiralled out of control.

"Did you see this?" Milo came jogging up the steps after me, his hand outstretched.

I glanced down at his phone, open to the Alstone High social media gossip page. Every single post was about the upcoming fight, odds of me knocking Asher out, malicious posts and images about Highnam Academy, and worst of all, derogatory comments about Asher that made my blood boil.

All morning, it was more of the same. I lost count of the number of people who had come up to me to wish me luck, to offer their thoughts on the fight, to tell me exactly what they thought of Asher.

It was too much. When the third person came up to me in the cafeteria, interrupting my lunch, I stood, shoving my chair back with a crash.

"I'm out of here," I announced to the suddenly silent table.

"You can't just leave halfway through the day." Milo stared up at me, his brows pulled together in concern.

"Watch me." Leaving my discarded tray on the table, I scooped my bag from the floor and turned in the direction of the doors.

I didn't stop walking until I reached my car. My phone was buzzing with texts, so I switched it off, throwing it onto the seat next to me before I roared out of the car park.

There was only one person who would understand this madness. And while everything in me rebelled at the thought of sharing my frustrations with him, while my brain reminded me that he was my rival in every way, I still found myself on the cliff road that led to Highnam.

I hadn't planned this, and I realised too late that there was a large number of students at Highnam Academy who would recognise my car. Slowing down as I reached the school, I circled around until I found a space on one of the residential side streets, where my car wouldn't be seen from the school. I still had my Alstone High uniform on, but my football kit was in the boot, along with one of my hoodies, so I switched out my clothing, ducking down in my seat and hoping that no one in the surrounding houses was watching me from their windows.

When I was dressed in less conspicuous clothes, I grabbed my phone and turned it on, then sent a text.

Me: Come outside

Then, I left my car and made my way to Highnam

Academy's gates. By the time I got there, I had a reply.

Loser: WTF? I'm in a class
Me: Leave it. I'm waiting outside
Loser: FFS. OK

A smile pulled at my lips. He was coming.

Less than five minutes later, Asher appeared from around the side of the school, jogging over to me. Glancing around us, he grabbed my arm and tugged me into the shadows, next to the wall at the side of the school.

"Are you insane?" he hissed. "What the fuck are you doing here? Shouldn't you be in school?"

"I walked out."

"Okaaaay. But why are you here?" He gave me one of his wary glances, his gorgeous eyes boring into me.

I scuffed the toe of my shoe on the ground, suddenly unsure. "Can you come for a drive?"

Blowing out a heavy breath, he nodded slowly. "I guess if you're going to make me skive off school for the afternoon, the least you can do is play my personal chauffeur."

"You wish," I shot back as I started heading back in the direction of my car. "Is there anywhere around here we could go?"

He chewed on his lip, falling into step next to me. "Uh...if you're trying to fly under the radar, probably not. Although...yeah. Maybe. I know a place."

We climbed into my car, and he helped himself to my satnav, inputting a destination about fifteen minutes away, then fiddling with the controls until he'd pulled up my Spotify.

"Don't take this as a compliment, but you have almost as

good taste in music as me." He hit one of my playlists, and MISSIO started blaring from the speakers.

Perfect. I tapped my fingers on the wheel as I directed the car out of the side street, pulling back onto the main road. "I won't hold my breath for a genuine compliment from you, don't worry."

He groaned, tipping his head back and screwing his eyes closed. "Fuck. Okay, this isn't a compliment to you, so don't get a big head. But I...fuck. Your car. *Your car.*"

"Yeah, yeah. I already know how much you love it."

He made a noise that might have been agreement, and I smiled to myself as we sped down the streets, leaving Highnam behind and heading down the coast road. The satnav eventually told me to turn off the coastal road, down a slope that ended in a small, empty car park at the bottom of the cliff. There was a tiny beach next to the car park, a mixture of sand and pebbles, and both the car park and the beach were empty. We couldn't be seen from the road down here, and I relaxed incrementally as I pulled up in front of a low stone wall that edged the car park.

When I got out, stretching, Asher stared at me over the top of the car. "Are you gonna tell me what this is all about?"

I nodded, and he disappeared from view. When I rounded the front of the car, I saw that he'd lowered himself to sit on the wall, his legs hanging over the edge, just out of reach of the sea that was lapping at the stone below us. Taking a seat next to him, I wondered at what my life had become this past week—voluntarily choosing to spend time with my rival. And everything else that had happened between us.

"I had to get out of school," I started, fixing my gaze on the horizon. "It was—"

"Fucking crazy?" Asher huffed a frustrated breath. "All anyone has spoken to me about is the fucking fight. All week it's been going on, and it's been even worse today. One of my teachers even brought it up, saying he hoped I'd put you in your place."

"Your teacher? That's next-level. But yeah, it's been...a lot. I had to get out, and I knew you, uh, I thought you might be experiencing the same thing."

I could feel his gaze on the side of my face. "It's fucked up, isn't it? I thought it might end with the fight, but I'm getting the feeling that when you lose, Alstone High are gonna want to hit us hard. They're already raging about the gym."

Familiar irritation stabbed at me. "I'm not going to lose," I bit out through clenched teeth. Taking a deep breath to calm myself, I forced myself to turn to meet his gaze. "I thought the same. I thought the fight might draw a line under it all, but the whole thing has gone too far. It's out of control now."

"Yeah." His mouth turned down, his shoulders slumping.

"Why did you refuse to shake my hand that first time we met?"

Asher's eyes widened. "At the football match?" When I nodded, he blew out a heavy breath. "Because of the look you gave me. Like I wasn't fucking good enough to be in your presence. I know you Alstone High boys like to lord it over us Highnam scum, but you made me feel like you thought I was completely fucking worthless. Then you started calling me by my football number, like I wasn't even deserving of being called by my name."

I reeled back as the low, bitter words fell from his lips, burning through me like acid. "Shit. I-I don't. I didn't realise."

"Whatever. It's in the past now." He turned to face the sea, his jaw set, but not before I caught the hurt shining in his eyes. There was a knot in my stomach that wouldn't loosen as my memory flashed to that match. He'd been cocky and overconfident, and it had instantly rubbed me up the wrong way. I'd—shit. Yeah, I'd definitely been the one to kick off the hostilities between us.

How did I make it right?

"Ten, look at me." I shifted closer until our sides were touching, but he remained statue-still, staring out to sea. Reaching out with a shaky hand, I cupped his jaw. He stiffened but otherwise didn't respond.

My thumb stroked across his skin. "*Asher.*"

His head flew around, and I lost my grip on his jaw, my hand falling to his shoulder. Shock was written all over his face as his wide brown eyes arrowed to mine.

I swallowed my pride and gathered my courage. "None of those things that you thought I was thinking were true. I thought you were an annoying, cocky fucker who needed to be taken down a peg or two. That was it. I was pissed off with you for refusing to shake my hand, and that's why I called you Ten."

A wry smile tugged at the corners of his lips. "An annoying, cocky fucker. Yeah, that's true." He shook his head. "Guess I can't put all the blame on you, though."

"No. You definitely take at least fifty percent of the blame." I curled my hand around the back of his neck. "Why don't we kiss and make up?"

A surprised laugh fell from his mouth, and the knot in my stomach loosened. His breath ghosted across my lips as he leaned into me. "You've already completely fucked my head up, so I guess another kiss isn't going to make it any worse."

When his lips slid across mine, I forgot everything else. The fight, our rivalry, the way I'd upset him—all of it was wiped from my mind. My world narrowed to the cool stone beneath me, the sharp, salty sea breeze, and Asher's hot, insistent mouth against my own.

His hand landed on my thigh as his lips moved to my throat, and I groaned, my growing erection hardening further as he squeezed my leg lightly. "Fuck. You make me so hard," he muttered into my neck, like he could read my mind.

I couldn't catch my breath. Placing my hand over the top of his, I moved them both up my thigh. He stilled, and hoping I wasn't making an even bigger mistake than the ones we'd made already, I kept up the movement until his hand was on my cock.

Exhaling shakily and letting go of his hand, I buried my face in his soft, messy hair. My heart was hammering, and my body was on fire.

He breathed shallowly against my throat, and I could feel his own heart pounding as fast as mine. His fingers twitched, and then he stroked down my cock, tentatively curling his fingers around the hard length.

"That feels so good." I swallowed thickly. "See how hard you make me."

Stroking back up again, he rubbed his thumb over the head, and the feel of his touch through the material of my shorts and underwear was so good, I moaned low in my throat, needing to touch him in return, to make him feel like I was.

"Touch me." His voice was wrecked. When I raised my

head, I saw his cock straining at the fabric of his trousers, and a jolt of lust hit me hard, my dick throbbing in his grip. Sliding my hand onto his thigh, I inched upwards until his erection was under my palm, hot and hard.

It wasn't enough. I needed to feel him properly, to blow his mind, to make him lose control.

My fingers went to the button of his trousers, and then I lowered his zipper. "I need to feel you," I rasped, choking on a moan as his stroking movements grew more confident, his mouth moving over my skin again, nipping and licking at my throat. "*Asher*. Don't stop."

He groaned as I eased my fingers inside his trousers and underwear, and when my fingers brushed over the head of his cock, he muttered a rough "fuck" against my skin. I lowered them further. His skin was warm and smooth under my fingertips as I curled my hand around his thick length.

"I want to touch you." His hand went to the band of my shorts, slipping underneath the fabric. "Tight," he mumbled, his fingers tugging against my underwear.

"Car?" I loosened my grip on him reluctantly. We were alone, but it was better to be safe. Plus, it was warmer in the car. "Come on."

We made it inside the car in under ten seconds, and I impatiently yanked down my shorts and underwear, watching as he did the same.

Fucking hell. I was into guys a lot more than I'd realised, or into Asher, at least. The sight of his erection, precum glistening at the tip, made my mouth water. He was slightly thicker than me but probably around the same length.

My gaze arrowed to his to see him staring at my cock through lowered lashes, a hot, heavy-lidded gaze. The sight of him looking at me like that sent another jolt of lust through my body, and I didn't want to waste any more time. Leaning over the centre console, I slanted my mouth over his while my hand curved around his hardness.

He touched me skin-to-skin for the first time, and my stroking movements faltered. Gripping my cock with the perfect pressure, like he knew exactly how I liked it, he slid his hand up, then down, then back up, his thumb rubbing carefully over the head again, smearing the precum around. It was a hundred times more sensitive without any fabric in the way and better than anything I'd ever felt before. "Yeah. Like that," I breathed against his lips.

"I didn't know it would be like this," he panted, thrusting up into my hand as I found a rhythm. "Fuck." His grip moved faster on my cock, and I groaned, my head falling back to my headrest as I gave myself over to my impending orgasm. His thrusts grew harder, and I tightened my grip, twisting my hand. It sent him over the edge, his cock pulsing beneath my fingers as his cum hit my hand and his stomach. It was the hottest thing I'd ever experienced in my life, and I came so hard that my vision blurred and I lost my breath.

"That was…" I gave up on words, my heart still hammering as I attempted to get air into my lungs.

The next second, his lips were brushing across mine. "Fucking amazing." He stilled against my mouth, and then, so quietly I almost missed it, he said my name for the first time.

"*Levi.*"

FIFTEEN
ASHER

The crowds were gathering, and every time I thought that was it, more people would appear. Everyone was riled up, ready for blood.

Too bad I wasn't.

I didn't want to fight Levi anymore.

After he'd dropped me back in Highnam, late Friday afternoon, I hadn't been able to get him off my mind. Whatever attraction, lust, and feelings I'd had towards any girl in the past paled into insignificance when I compared it to the way he affected me. What that meant for the future, and for my sexuality, I didn't have a clue. All I knew was that my mind was completely fucking twisted over Levi Woodford.

We hadn't spoken or texted since Friday, not that I was expecting to, and I could more or less guarantee that he was probably feeling just as shaken as I was by everything that had gone down between us. Space to think was what we both needed, but here we were, about to face each other in front of a massive throng of people who all wanted one or both of us to pay.

My head wasn't in this fight, and I knew that the only way I'd be able to get through it would be to totally switch off, to let my body do the work, to shut off everything he made me feel and to just see him as another opponent. I'd fought in the bowl plenty of times before—we both had—so it wasn't like the fight itself would be a new experience.

The atmosphere in the crowds was new, though.

Over in our corner on the left side of the bowl, Danny finished wrapping my hands, then shoved a mouthguard at me. "He'll go for your face, and you don't wanna lose a tooth."

"Yeah," I mumbled, my attention focused on the far side of the bowl, where I caught a glimpse of ash-brown hair.

"Hey, mate, you okay? You can pull out of this if you want. Or I can take your place—I wouldn't mind messing up Levi's face. Probably improve it."

"You're not touching his face," I snapped, yanking the mouthguard out of his grip. He stared at me in shock, and I panicked, struggling to recover. "I mean, no. I'll fight him. Sorry. Got a lot on my mind at the minute. Work and school shit, and now this on top of it all."

He nodded, easily accepting my excuse, and I felt a spike of guilt. I hated lying to my friends, but there was no way I was going to tell anyone that I'd been messing around with my enemy.

Clapping me on the shoulder, he gave me a quick, reassuring grin. "You'll be fine when you get in there. You can beat him, no problem."

Danny's words penetrated the fog in my brain, and I forced myself to remember what this fight was all about. It wasn't even personal anymore, not for me, anyway. It was about proving that Highnam Academy could hold their own against Alstone High. That we were their equals, despite our differences in social status and wealth. If I lost this, I'd be letting down everyone that was counting on me to put Alstone High in their place.

I had to win.

I had to get the best of Levi.

The previous fight was finished, and I made my way to the edge of the bowl. As soon as I appeared, the noise from the crowd increased to deafening levels, spiking when my opponent appeared on the opposite edge. Our eyes met across the bowl, and tension crackled between us. He was dressed the same as me, tracksuit bottoms and a tight T-shirt, his hands wrapped. Clasping my mouthguard, I slid down into the bowl and went to the middle, where the fight referee was waiting. If I looked up, I knew I'd see people crowded all around the edge, legs dangling over the side, staring down at us. But down here, it was easy to ignore, focusing only on my opponent.

Mack, the guy acting as the referee and organiser of the fight nights, shook both our hands. "You know the rules. First to tap out loses." He stepped back and climbed out of the bowl, and then it was just me and Levi.

I licked my lips, clenching and unclenching my fists. "This isn't personal."

Levi shook his head, a short, jerky movement. "It's always been personal."

"If that's the way you want it to be. Show me what you've got, *Seven*." Stung, I shoved my mouthguard in.

A spark of remorse flashed in his eyes, and he took a single step closer. His voice was so low I almost couldn't hear him. "I need you to hate me, Ten."

He lifted his mouthguard to his lips, sliding it in, then nodded once.

The whistle blew from above us, and he lunged for me.

Normally when I fought in the bowl, my opponent would become a faceless blur, my mind emptied of every thought except for the fight itself, but something in my subconscious kept reminding me that this wasn't just any other opponent. Maybe it was the time we'd spent together lately, fighting, pinning each other, and everything else, but it felt like we anticipated every single movement the other made. Whenever Levi got me in a hold, I broke free. Whenever I thought I had the upper hand, he'd surprise me with a move that switched the balance of power back to him.

I reeled backwards when I received a glancing blow off my chin, hard enough to rattle my teeth. Pushing my body harder than I'd ever had to in any fight, I retaliated with a roundhouse kick that made him stagger to the side. He instantly recovered, lunging at me and getting in a punch to my midsection that left me gasping for breath. I countered his move with a jab to his ribs, then another until he got me in a headlock.

Breaking free of his hold, I gasped in a lungful of air, then hit him with a right hook, straight to the side of his face. We exchanged blow after blow, grappling, kicking, and punching until both of us were dripping with sweat and pain radiated through my entire body. I was starting to tire, and Levi was relentless, like a machine, coming at me without showing any sign of slowing down.

For the first time, doubt crept into my mind. Maybe I wouldn't be able to win this.

From above us came the sound of the whistle, distant over the ringing in my ears. My lungs burning, I pulled back from Levi, locking my knees to force myself to stay upright as I gasped for breath.

Mack jogged over to us. "Time's up. I'm gonna have to declare a draw. We can set up a rematch."

I could just about manage a thumbs up. The sweat was dripping in my eyes, and I rubbed my hand across my face.

"No rematch. That's it." Levi spoke hoarsely, breathing hard.

No rematch? Shock raced through me, my heart pounding even harder than it had been, sending spots dancing across my vision.

"Asher? That okay with you?" Mack studied me. "There's gonna be backlash."

"Yeah," I panted. "No rematch."

"Your funeral." He grabbed both of our hands and lifted them in the air.

The boos were deafening.

Hands helped us out of the bowl, and Danny was there waiting for me, taking my mouthguard and handing me a towel. I ripped off my T-shirt and unwrapped my hands as quickly as I could. My knuckles were split and bloodied, despite their protection, and I winced as Danny poured cold water over them.

"Thanks, mate." I grabbed the water and tipped it over my head as the rest of the football team crowded around me, giving me words of support and telling me I hadn't let them down. It surprised me, since the boos had been so loud, but it appeared that there was still a residual high from our stunt on Fright Night. I doubted that would be the case when I showed up at school the next day.

The crowds dispersed quickly, leaving me alone with the football team surrounding me. Danny handed me my backpack containing my phone, car keys, and a hoodie. "Ready to get out of here?"

"Yeah." I hurt everywhere, and I needed a shower.

As a group, we all headed down into the underpass to cross over to where we'd parked our cars. Danny lowered his voice, glancing around us as he moved closer to me. "Why no rematch?"

I had the same question, but for now, I gave him my own answer. "Because it's never-ending. I'm fucking tired, Dan."

Because he was my best mate and a good guy, he just nodded. "It shouldn't be all up to you. We're all involved. Next time, I'll fight Milo."

It *should* all be up to me. I'd been the one to kick all this shit off, along with Levi. We were the team captains, so we had to take responsibility. People looked to us for guidance.

"Appreciate it," was all I said, giving him a nudge, then immediately regretting it when he nudged me back, right on one of the fresh bruises decorating my body. "Fuck, I didn't think I was gonna last out there. A minute longer, and I probably would've gone down."

"Yeah..." His voice was thoughtful. "I dunno, I might be wrong. But it looked to me like Levi was holding back a bit, right at the end."

"He'd better fucking not have. There's no honour in a draw when one person didn't play fair."

"Like I said, I might be wrong. No one else said anything about it."

We reached our cars, thoughts swirling through my mind. I had questions for Levi, and I knew I wouldn't be able to sleep until I confronted him. Lucky for me, we'd come in separate cars, so as soon as everyone disappeared, I headed in the direction of Levi's house.

It was time to get some answers.

SIXTEEN
LEVI

The sound of running water coming from my bathroom alerted me to Asher's presence. Turning on my heel, I headed into the guest bathroom to shower. I winced as the water pummelled my bruises, wondering how badly he was going to react when he confronted me.

When I was showered and dressed in loose, soft grey cotton shorts, I dragged my aching body back into my room to find Asher at my desk, staring at his phone. The second I appeared in the doorway, he planted his phone on the desk, rising to his feet and crossing over to me. His dark hair was wet from the shower, and all he was wearing was a tight pair of black boxer briefs.

I sucked in a breath, my dick instantly reacting despite my body's pain and exhaustion. He looked so good.

Easing the door shut behind me, since my parents were actually home for once, although both of them were heavy sleepers, I drank him in.

"Ash—"

He lifted his hand to stop me speaking, his eyes darkening as he glowered at me. "I don't want to talk."

My heart hammered inside my chest, my stomach churning as I stared at him. Had the fight messed everything up between us? "But—"

"Later." Taking a step closer, he slid his hand onto my jaw. His grip was light and careful as he tilted my head, examining my face. "Fuck," he muttered, the pads of his fingers ghosting over the bruising skin on my cheek. Without saying another word, he gripped my wrist and tugged me towards my en suite. The room was steamy from his shower, a towel slung haphazardly over the towel rail, and the sink almost overflowing with what looked like ice cubes.

My gaze caught on the empty bag on the counter. Yep. Ice—clearly, he'd helped himself to the contents of my parents' freezer.

He silently dipped a large washcloth in the sink, wrapping it around a handful of ice cubes, then lifted it to my face. I gritted my teeth as the chill hit my skin, but I knew it would ease any swelling.

Holding it to my face, his gaze tracked over the rest of my body as he catalogued all my injuries. "Not too bad," he murmured, directing me to hold the ice to my cheek while he turned me around, his hand skimming over my back with an almost clinical touch as he examined me. When he was finally done, he took a step away, slumping back against the counter, his gaze shuttered.

There was a knot in my stomach as I took in his defeated posture. I stepped up to him, and mimicking his movements, checked him over for injuries. My hand running over his warm, clean skin had my dick reacting far too inappropriately for the situation, given that he was clearly upset with me and in pain, so I moved away from him and carefully placed my makeshift ice pack on the side of the sink. Digging out another washcloth, I assembled a makeshift ice pack for him, holding it to his jaw.

"I can do it. Use yours."

Deciding it was best to do what he wanted for now, I let him take the ice pack from me and lifted mine back to my cheek.

The silence stretched between us. Asher lowered his gaze to the floor, keeping it fixed there until both our ice packs had melted. Suddenly moving, he swiped the towel from the rail, throwing the washcloth into the sink and then used the towel to wipe away the icy liquid on his skin. When he was finished, he threw me the towel without a word and disappeared out of the door.

When I re-entered my bedroom, I found him standing in the centre of the room, a resolute expression on his face as his eyes met mine.

"You owe me some answers, Seven." His jaw tightened. "I don't know if I want to kiss you or punch you right now."

He still wanted to kiss me, and I wasn't about to let that opportunity pass me by.

Taking a leaf out of his book, I backed him towards the bed until the backs of his knees hit the side of the mattress. "You can do both, if you want to, as long as you're prepared for me to give you the same treatment." Then I shoved at him, sending him backwards onto the bed with me on top of him.

He threw me off straight away, kicking up and launching himself so he was fully on the bed, then he struck out, grabbing me around the waist and pulling me to him. Rolling us, he pinned me down, like I knew he would.

"What happened tonight?" He planted his elbows either side of my head, staring down at me.

"We fought, and we drew."

"Don't play stupid." Taking my lip between his teeth, he bit down, a warning that he wasn't going to play nice if I didn't give him the answers he needed.

"Okay. Can you get off me, though? You bruised me all over."

"You did the same," he muttered, but he rolled off me anyway, settling on his side with a wince. I mimicked his position, and he hooked his leg around mine, tugging me closer so our bodies were aligned. "Better. Now you're in easy reach if I need to…whatever."

I reached out, threading my fingers through his damp hair, pushing it back from his face. "Such a mess."

"What is your obsession with my hair?" He traced a finger down my arm. "Come on, Seven. There's no point trying to change the subject. I need answers."

Releasing my grip on his hair, I sighed. "Okay. But you're not going to like it."

His body stiffened, so I curled my arm around his back, angling my head forwards to place a kiss to his unsmiling mouth. "How are you so sexy even when you're in a mood?"

A tiny, unwilling smile appeared on his lips. "Stop trying to butter me up, and get to the point."

"Okay, okay." My hand started tracing circles on his back. "I knew that if I met Asher in the bowl, I wouldn't be able to go through with that fight. I needed you to be Ten. My rival. I needed you to hate me. There was no way either of us would have been able to get out of fighting each other, so I did what I had to."

He sucked his lip between his teeth, his brows pulling

together as he considered my words. When he nodded slowly, I let out a relieved breath, moving my hand from his back to cradle his jaw. His stubble rasped underneath the pads of my fingers, and I suddenly wondered how it would feel between my thighs.

My dick liked the idea, that was for sure. On the pretence of shifting on the bed, I angled my hips closer to him.

He smirked at me.

"I know what you're doing." His hand snaked down between us to cup my bulge. "Final question. And bear in mind that I've literally got you by the balls right now. Were you holding back at the end of the fight?"

This was the part he wasn't going to be happy with, and I was actually scared for my dick. "Please let go of me, and I'll answer."

Immediately releasing me, Asher rolled onto his back, flinging his arm over his face. "Fucking seriously? I wanted it to be a fair fight. How am I supposed to show my face now, knowing you engineered the outcome? Knowing you would've beaten me?"

His words were low and angry, but the hurt was clear.

Pulling his arm away from his face, I gripped his jaw again, holding his head in position. "Listen to me. I want this to be over, don't you? A draw was the only way it was going to happen. I wasn't even holding back, not until about fifteen seconds before Mack blew his whistle. There was a point then where I could've taken advantage and knocked you down, but I didn't, because we needed that draw. There was no other outcome that would have been acceptable. We needed to publicly end this rivalry between us, and now our part in this whole thing is over."

"It's not over." His arm shot up, yanking my hand away

from his jaw. "Do you even realise what kind of shit you're going to walk into tomorrow?"

"Yeah, but we won't have to fight again. I don't want to do that with you anymore, Asher."

When I said his name, all the fight went out of him, leaving only the hurt. I hated seeing that expression on his face, knowing that I'd been the one to put it there.

"I'm sorry. I thought I was doing the right thing." My voice shook. Fuck. I hadn't realised just how important it was that he forgave me until right then. "I don't want to go back to being enemies again."

His gaze softened. "I still really want to punch you. But I don't want to be your enemy anymore."

"Go on, then." I moved onto my back, shifting away from him. Steeling myself against the blow, I squeezed my eyes shut. "I'll let you get one hit in for free."

A huff of breath skated across my mouth as the bed dipped. "You're insane," he murmured, and then his lips were on mine.

My bruises were forgotten as we kissed and kissed, rolling across the bed, flipping each other over, until we were panting into each other's mouths, grinding our hips into one another.

I couldn't get enough of him.

"I really want to fuck you." Asher raised his head from my neck a while later, his hand inside my shorts, rubbing over my hard cock. I was so close to the edge, but every time I thought I was getting there, he pulled away. Sadistic bastard.

"Fuck, Ash. I want to fuck you, too." I pulled his lip between my teeth, then dragged him into another kiss, all teeth and tongues as I bucked against him, my hands gripping onto his ass as he ground his cock against my thigh. "You need to be naked, now."

"Yeah," he agreed, sliding his hand off my cock and pulling my shorts down. As I kicked them off, he yanked down his own underwear, and finally, there was nothing between us. I leaned over to kiss him, but he stopped me with a hand to my chest. "Let me look at you."

Rising up onto his elbows, his gaze tracked the length of my body. "You're so fucking hot." He climbed to his knees and straddled me, lining up his bare dick with mine and taking them both in his hand. Biting down on his lip, he stared down at me as he began a steady movement, up and down. "Fuck," he groaned when my hips jerked, the hot slide of his cock against mine and the friction of his hand sending me straight back to the edge again.

"So good." I reached my hands out to his thighs, needing to touch him. "Don't stop."

"I, uh, researched." His hand moved faster, his cheeks flushing. "I wanted to see if…if…" The words died in his throat as my stomach muscles seized up, my dick jerking in his grip, coming all over his hand and his cock. Teeth clamping down on his lip again, he used my cum to lube up his dick, and it was the hottest thing I'd ever seen. Four short strokes later, and his mouth fell open, the sexiest low moan tearing from his throat as he found his own release.

He used my shorts to give us both a cursory wipe over, then threw them somewhere on the floor and collapsed on the bed next to me, his breaths gradually evening out.

"You wanted to see what?" I rested my head on my elbow, the fingers of my other hand curling around his.

He picked at a loose thread on my duvet, his cheeks darkening even further. "If it was something I was interested in. Gay sex. Sex with you."

"What was the verdict?"

An annoyed huff escaped him. "I know you know that I've liked everything we've done, Levi. And in case you want me to spell it out for you, when I was saying I wanted to fuck you, I didn't just mean in the ways we've already tried. I meant my dick in you, or yours in me, if that's what you want."

"You said my name again." I leaned forwards, my mouth sliding across his. "Does this mean we're friends?"

"Frenemies, maybe." He smiled against my lips.

Letting go of his hand, I punched him lightly in the arm. "You're a dick."

"So are you." He glowered at me, rubbing his arm.

Pulling him to me, I tugged his bottom lip between my teeth, which turned into another kiss when he opened his mouth to me. When it ended, we were both breathless. "I want what you want. To fuck. But I..." I swallowed hard. "I don't just want to be your gay experiment."

Asher's gaze turned serious as he drew back to look at me. "It's not like that. I mean, yeah, I do want to experiment. I want to try new things. But not for that reason." He turned away from me then, burying his face in the pillow. Although his voice was now muffled, I could still hear him clearly, and my heart rate sped up at his words. "I want to try them with *you*. Because I like you."

"You like me?" I attempted to pry his head from the pillow so I could see his face, but he turned over again so he had his back to me. "Asher. Come here." Lightly scraping my teeth across his shoulder, I ran my hand down his arm coaxingly.

"How the fuck did this even happen?" he asked, his tone

soft and completely bewildered. "I just don't get it."

"I've been asking myself the same thing ever since Fright Night." Propping myself up on my elbow, I put my mouth to his ear. "So we're both on the same page, you're not my gay experiment, either. You've reinforced some stuff I was working out about myself, in fact. And…and I like you, too, even though you irritate the fuck out of me at least sixty percent of the time."

Finally, he turned to face me. "Only sixty percent? Guess I'll have to try harder."

"I'm already regretting this."

A wide smile curved across his lips. "Liar." He kissed me once, chastely, then rolled away from me. "I'd better go. It's getting late, and we've both got shit to face tomorrow."

"Can't wait." I lay back with a groan.

"Wanna meet up afterwards and compare notes?" Opening my drawers, he helped himself to yet more of my clothes without even asking.

"Yes."

He smiled at my instant response, pulling on a pair of distressed jeans and a pale blue T-shirt that suited him way better than me. "Better not tell anyone you're fraternising with the enemy."

"There's no way I'm telling anyone. You'd better not, either. Why do my clothes look better on you than me?"

Crossing back to the bed, he leaned down, sliding his fingers into my hair, and kissed me again. "Because you wanna fuck me, and therefore, you're biased when you look at me." One last kiss, and he straightened up. "See you tomorrow."

"Yeah. Good luck."

"You too." Easing the door open, he disappeared from

view, the door softly clicking shut behind him.

SEVENTEEN
ASHER

We didn't meet up on Monday. I got pulled in to work, and again on Tuesday. On Wednesday Levi's friends went over to his house, so there was no chance of us seeing each other then. We texted a bit, general commiserations about the reactions to our fight, although it sounded like Levi had it worse than me. Not that anyone had dared to say anything to him outright. In my school, the football team had my back, working overtime to spread images and videos from our pranks, reminding everyone that even though the fight had ended up in a draw, we were still on top. What shocked me the most was that a lot of people seemed to think that it was impressive I'd lasted so long against Levi, especially with his reputation as a decent fighter.

While all that took some of the pressure off me, I wanted to see him, needed to check if he was okay. Plus, yeah, if I admitted it, I just wanted to see him, whatever the circumstances. Still couldn't get my head around it all, still no idea how it had even happened, but I was into him. End of. It was a fucking hard situation, because I couldn't even mention him to anyone in case they got suspicious.

I finally got my chance to see him on Thursday, when we were both free. At last. Closing my front door, I jogged the few steps to the street, turning in the direction of the lock-up where I parked my car for a small monthly fee.

"Asher!"

Pausing with my hand on the car door, I looked up to see Danny and Talia standing at the entrance to the lock-up. Fuck. I hoped they didn't ask me where I was going. "Alright?"

"Where are you off to?" Talia shifted her bag on her shoulder, slipping out from under Danny's arm and taking a step closer to my car.

"Going for a drive," I said, which was technically true.

"Want some company?"

"Uh, not really. Nothing personal."

They both eyed me with suspicion, so I added, "Just need to get on the road for a bit, drive around and clear my head."

Talia came to stand right in front of me, that suspicious look still all over her face. "You're not going to do anything stupid, are you?"

Define stupid. Does meeting up with your mortal enemy-slash-boy you're way too fucking into count?

"Talia. You know me better than that."

"She does, mate, and that's why we know you're up to something." Danny strolled over to join her in front of me. "If it's illegal, I want in. Don't even think about leaving me out."

The thought of them knowing who I was meeting up

with was too much. My head was a mess—I couldn't even explain it to myself, so how could I explain it to them? Plus, I had no idea how they'd react to the fact that I was apparently now into guys as well as girls...or one guy, at least. And his identity...they'd both have a big, big problem with that.

Far better to stay quiet until I worked out what this was between me and Levi. And until all the rivalry drama had died down. If it ever did.

"I'm not doing anything illegal. I'm going for a drive." With that, I swung open my car door and slid inside, locking the doors behind me. I lowered the window, leaning my elbow on the edge of the window frame. "See you in school tomorrow. We'll catch up properly at the weekend."

Swinging out into the road, I knew they wouldn't let this go, but at least I'd bought myself some time.

When I reached the car park at Alstone's pier, I spotted Levi's McLaren straight away, parked across two spaces. The momentary flare of annoyance disappeared when I realised that I'd probably do the same if I owned his car. It didn't mean I wasn't going to mention it to him, though.

After parking as far away from his car as possible, I managed to make it into the cinema undetected, keeping the hood of my hoodie up just in case. Levi was waiting for me over by the pick 'n' mix selection, also with his hood up, his gaze bouncing around the foyer, scanning everyone that entered.

"Hi." There was no way I could stop my grin when I came to a stop in front of him, and he smiled at me, his eyes lighting up.

"Hi. I got tickets, and there's no one I recognise around." He held up his phone.

"You already got them?" Immediately on the defensive,

I narrowed my eyes at him. "I don't need your charity; I can get my own."

Lowering his voice, he frowned at me. "It's not charity. I wanted to get them, okay?"

"Why? It's not like this is a date." I took in the look on his face. "Is it?"

He shrugged, dropping his gaze to the floor, shoving his phone and his hands into his pockets.

My stomach flipped. "Levi." Taking a step closer, I reached out and touched his arm briefly, the most I dared to do out in the open like this. "If it's a date, then I'm paying for the snacks."

His eyes flicked back to mine, his expression hesitant. The fact that he seemed so unsure for once increased my confidence somehow.

"Yeah, it's a date," I confirmed with a decisive nod. "What do you want? Sweet or salted popcorn? Nachos? Sweets? All of them? We can share if you want."

"Whatever. I like salted popcorn, but I know you've got a sweet tooth." He flashed me a quick, tentative grin, and I had a sudden flashback of him helping himself to my candy floss at Fright Night.

"It's all about the ratio." Picking up one of the cardboard tubs next to the pick 'n' mix, I studied the selection in front of me. "We have salted popcorn, and we balance it out with sweets. But not those foam bananas. Or the chocolate-coated raisins."

He grabbed one of the scoops and opened the lid of the section with the fizzy cola bottles. "These are my favourite."

"But they're my favourite."

Rolling his eyes, he huffed. "We're both allowed to like the same thing, Ash."

"I like you saying my name." The words weren't supposed to come out, but apparently, they did. He shifted closer to me, his voice dropping to a husky whisper.

"You'll like it even better when I say it later."

"Fuck, don't say things like that when we're in public." I moved away from him before I ended up doing something completely inadvisable. "Who are you, and what have you done with my angry nemesis?"

"It's still me." Scooping up the cola bottles, he filled the cardboard tub all the way to the top. "Just like you're still your usual irritating self."

"Speaking of irritating…" I shoved a lid on the tub of cola bottles, then headed in the direction of the counter. "Some rich twat parked his flash car across two spaces in the car park. Did you see?"

"I must've missed it." He was looking at the menu screen behind the cashier, but I caught his smile. "What are we getting? A large Coke and a large salted popcorn?"

"If you want to share, yeah. These, too." Sliding the sweets across the counter to the cashier, I grinned. "You—"

"Levi!"

Next to me, Levi stiffened, and his eyes shot to mine, panic written all over his face. Slowly turning around, I was met with the hostile gazes of three guys I recognised from the Alstone High football team.

Great.

I was panicking inside, too, but I wasn't going to make Levi's life any harder than it already had been since our fight.

"What is this, dickheads' day out? First I run into your asshole captain, now you lot show up?" Giving Levi a shove that he was unprepared for, making him stumble, I pushed past the group of glaring guys, ignoring the cashier's amused expression.

There was plenty I could've said, but I didn't want to antagonise the situation. Best to get out of there as quick as possible.

I headed out of the side exit into the alleyway that led around the back of the cinema building. Pulling my hood down, I took a seat on the wall that marked a small private parking area. Then I pulled out my phone and waited.

A few minutes later, my phone buzzed.

Seven: Where are you?
Me: Round the back. Go out the side exit

He appeared a couple of minutes later, stalking over to me with a look of frustration on his face. Slamming the tub of cola bottles down on the wall next to me, he kicked out at the wall. "Fuck!"

"Levi." Widening my legs, I cocked my head at him, and he came to stand in front of me. I closed my thighs, trapping him there.

His arms came around me, but tension thrummed through his body. "I should've known that someone one of us knew would be there."

I pulled him closer, tugging his hood down so I could see his expression properly. "What did they say to you?" Before he could reply, I slanted my mouth over his, because I couldn't wait any longer to kiss him. He opened up to me straight away, throwing his frustrations into our kiss. Gripping the back of my skull, he kissed me hard, biting at my lips, pressing his body right up to mine.

A lightbulb clicked on in my brain, and I shoved him

backwards, lunging off the wall after him and pushing him until his back crashed against the cinema building. "I know what you need." My mouth went to his throat, and I sank my teeth in. "Come on, baby. You know I can handle it."

A growl tore from his throat, and he broke out of my hold, twisting away and yanking my arms behind my back as he pushed me face first into the building. His body was pressing into my back, and his breaths were harsh and fast in my ear. "I think I like this position."

I didn't let him enjoy it for long. Now that we were... whatever we were to each other, I had a whole set of new weapons in my arsenal. "Mmm." I tilted my head to the side, baring my neck to him, and as he took the bait, I snapped out of his grip, spinning to the side and throwing myself against his back. Now our positions were reversed.

When his body shuddered beneath mine, I forgot why I'd started this in the first place.

"Fighting you makes me so fucking hard," I panted, grinding my cock against his ass. Snaking my hand around him, I reached down to rub over the front of his jeans. "Seems I'm not the only one."

"Asher." He groaned low in his throat. I gave him space to turn around to face me, and then I kissed him properly, one arm curled around the back of his neck and the other around his waist. When we broke apart, I met his soft, smoky gaze. Fuck, the way he was looking at me...

My heart was pounding, my dick was hard, and butterflies or moths or whatever that fluttering thing was were going mad inside me.

I *really* liked this guy. And I didn't want to do anything to fuck it up.

There was still a tension to his body that had been there

from the beginning, and I figured he could do with some proper stress relief. "Let's talk about this later. Is it safe to go back inside?"

"I think so. They were going to see a different movie."

"Good. Because I want to see if I can get away with something."

"What?"

"Something. We should go in separately. Text me the ticket so I can scan my own, and I'll get the drink and popcorn and meet you in there, yeah?"

Levi nodded. "Okay. It's probably safer." Digging his phone out of his jeans pocket, he texted me the ticket details, then picked up the tub of cola bottles. "See you in there."

I waited until he'd disappeared around the corner and then took my time strolling back inside, ordering the popcorn and drink. When I entered Screen 12, it was almost empty, just two other people sitting about halfway up the rows of seats and Levi right at the back.

"You chose well." I slid into the seat next to him, placing the drink in the cup-holder and handing him the popcorn. As I stretched my legs out in front of me, the lights dimmed, and the first of the trailers began playing.

"I know. This movie's been out for ages, so I knew it wouldn't be busy."

"So." I slid my hand onto his thigh, lowering my voice as I tilted my head closer to his. "I always wanted to mess around with someone in the back row of the cinema."

A gasp fell from his lips as I ran my palm all the way up his thigh. I flicked open the top button of his jeans.

"Ash…"

"I want to suck you off. Are you gonna let me?" I nipped at his ear, enjoying his shiver as I continued flicking open the buttons of his fly.

He turned to stare at me with wide eyes, and his tongue darted out to lick his lips. "What you do to me...*fuck*. I'm not going to turn down a blowjob from you."

"Good. Give me some room."

When he shoved his jeans down and widened his legs, I took another quick glance around to make sure no one else had shown up, then sank to my knees on the floor, positioning myself between his thighs. I eased his hard cock out of his underwear, watching as he bit down on his lip to stifle a groan, gripping onto the popcorn tightly with one hand and the other clenching the armrest of his chair.

This was good. He was on edge already. This was going to be a new experience for both of us, being with a guy, but I wanted to make it good for him. Curling my fingers around his hard length, I lowered my head to his cock, my other hand resting on his thigh for balance. "Don't get popcorn in my hair," I cautioned before I closed my mouth around him, taking my first taste.

He was warm and hard beneath my tongue, his thighs tensed either side of me as he held himself completely still, letting me get used to the fact that I was sucking a dick for the first time in my life.

Running my free hand over his thigh, I dragged my tongue over the head, tasting the slight bitterness of his precum, hearing another stifled groan from above me.

Then his hand was tugging at my hair. "Wait. I need to put this popcorn down, otherwise it will actually end up in your hair."

I smiled at the urgency in his tone, hearing the rustling of the bag above me but keeping my focus on my task, which was to blow his mind with my newly discovered dick-sucking skills. He must've put it down somewhere, because both of his hands slid into my hair as I licked and sucked the head of his cock, then lowered myself to take him deeper.

Since it was my first time doing this, I took my cues from him, listening to his gasps and pants, the way his fingers would flex on my head, how his thighs would jerk when I sucked harder, deeper. My hand that had been resting on his thigh snaked down between his legs, lightly rolling his balls the way I knew I liked, and when I pressed a finger to his taint, he jerked up so hard that I choked, my eyes watering as his dick hit the back of my throat without any warning.

I loved it. Blowing his cock, blowing his mind. Bringing him pleasure, making him forget all the shit that waited for us in the outside world.

"Ash, I'm—"

Pulling off him and taking a gasped breath, I met his gaze. "Come down my throat. I want it all."

"Oh, fuck," he choked out, thrusting up when I took him into my mouth again. What could have only been about five seconds later, his dick pulsed in my mouth, cum hitting my throat faster than I could swallow.

His hands released my head, and he handed me the bunch of napkins I'd grabbed with my popcorn. As he came down from his high, I cleaned up and wiped off my mouth. I rolled my tongue experimentally. "Hmm. I think I could get used to the taste."

He let out a shuddering laugh. "I hope so. I don't want that experience to be a one-off."

Straightening up, I sank back into my seat, adjusting my erection in my jeans. He made me so hard, and sucking his cock had turned me on more than I could've imagined. I wasn't going to ask him to reciprocate, though. This whole thing was uncharted territory for us both.

But Levi being Levi, he didn't miss anything. He slid out of his seat and onto mine, straddling my thighs. The movie had started playing by this point, but neither of us had been paying any attention. There were explosions blasting out from the speakers, but my whole world had narrowed to him leaning down to nip at my bottom lip, then sliding his tongue into my mouth. The fact that I knew he could taste himself made me groan, my cock pounding as he slid his hand down between us.

"I want to do that to you," he whispered against my lips, his hand stroking over my hardness. "Can I?"

"Fuck, yes. *Please*."

He got on his knees and gave me the messiest, but best, blowjob of my entire life.

We actually managed to watch the second half of the movie, and thankfully the plot was non-existent, so it was easy enough to pick up, all the budget going on the special effects rather than the screenplay. After it had finished we walked out separately, then met back at my car so we could talk. The car park was emptying out, and I'd parked right in the far corner, but I made both of us sit in the back seats since the rear windows were tinted black, and no one would be able to see in unless they put their face right up against the glass.

"Tell me what they said." I leaned against the side window, stretching my legs across the back seat, and Levi did the same on the opposite side, his legs tangling with mine as he faced me.

"They wanted to know why I was at the cinema on my own. I made up a story about being stood up, saying I was just leaving. I think they bought it."

"What about school? What's that been like?"

He took a deep breath, and it all spilled out of him. How people were still expecting retaliation for Fright Night, and they weren't happy with the fact that our fight had been a draw, and he was being pressured to act. "No one's dared to say anything to my face, but it's all anyone's been talking about. You know I'm not going to do anything else to you, but I'm worried…if I say or do nothing, then someone else might take matters into their own hands."

"I can handle it, whatever happens," I promised him. "You don't need to worry about me."

The distressed expression remained on his face, so I untangled my legs from his and carefully shifted across the cramped space so that I was face to face with him. "I can handle it."

His hands slid up, stroking across the back of my neck. "I don't want you to have to handle it. I don't want to be worrying if someone's going to jump you. I…I care about you."

"Levi…" I buried my face in his throat, unable to meet his eyes. "I care about you," I mumbled against his hoodie. His chest rose and fell in a deep exhale as he ran his hand down my back.

There was nothing else either of us could say.

EIGHTEEN
ASHER

Three...two...one...

"What the fuck!" Right on cue, Danny's whole body jerked, his head shooting up and his eyes flying open as I fell about laughing next to him.

"I knew slamming my textbooks on the table would wake you up." I gave him a wide grin, to which he responded by giving me the middle finger. Shaking my head at him, I tutted. "You really shouldn't be sleeping in class, mate."

He gave me a sheepish smile. "Yeah...Talia kept me up late last night."

"I knew it." I glanced past him to Talia, who just shrugged and mouthed, *Not my fault*.

"Quiet!" Mr. Allen roared from the front of the classroom, his gaze fixed on us both. "One more word out of either of you, and you'll be in detention!"

"The man's deluded." Danny leaned back in his chair, swinging it onto its back legs. "He wouldn't dare to make us miss football training for detention."

"Yeah, that's not gonna—"

As if in slow motion, I watched Danny's chair tip backwards with him in it, landing on the floor with a crash. I couldn't have stopped my laughter even if I'd wanted to; seeing his expression of shock as he went down was fucking hilarious. Talia buried her face in her arms, her shoulders shaking, and as Danny clambered to his feet, rubbing his head, I couldn't even breathe through my laughter. Danny glared at me, but then his lips twitched, and a laugh burst out of him.

"Asher! Danny! Detention!"

Fuck.

At the end of the school day, while all our friends were training with the team, Danny and I were instead stuck in a classroom with Mr. Allen and eight other students who had managed to incur the wrath of one of the teachers at some point during the day. Our pleas had fallen on deaf ears, even with Dave and Mick intervening on behalf of the team. According to Mr. Allen, we were "two disruptive nuisances, who needed to be taught a lesson."

The hour's detention dragged endlessly, and twenty minutes in, I surreptitiously balanced my phone on my thigh under the table, opening up my text conversation with Levi.

Me: Tell me your afternoon is better than mine

A reply came through almost straight away, but I had to wait until Mr. Allen's attention was diverted before I glanced at my screen again.

Seven: What have you done?

Me: Why do you assume I've done anything?
Seven: Am I wrong?
Me: FU. I'm in detention
Seven: I knew it
Me: Don't act smug
Seven: Want to meet up after or do you have to work?

"Who are you texting?" Danny leaned across to my desk, trying to get a look at my phone screen. Nosy bastard.

"No one you know."

"Oh, it's a girl, is it?" A knowing glint appeared in his eye. "Let me guess. Lucy Penrose." He threw out the name of one of the girls in our year, a girl I couldn't even remember speaking to before.

"What? No! Why would you think that?"

He shrugged. "She's always staring at you."

Was she? "Can't say I've noticed, mate."

Mr. Allen chose that moment to climb to his feet, pacing the room, and Danny moved away from me, saving me from his interrogation for now. Fuck, if he knew who I was texting…

I returned my attention to my phone.

Me: I'm free
Seven: Do you want to meet up somewhere? Or come to mine?
Me: I'll come to yours. I'm hungry so you better feed me
Seven: What do I get in return?

Several pornographic images flashed through my brain, and I shifted in my seat.

Me: DO NOT GIVE ME A BONER IN DETENTION
Seven: Not my fault. Answer my question
Me: I'll suck your cock

As soon as I hit Send, I had a moment of panic, and my gaze darted to Danny, who was texting on his own phone. I slumped back in my seat, relieved. Him thinking I was texting a girl was one thing, but if he saw I'd sent a message saying *I'll suck your cock*… There was no way I could explain that one away.

When I dared to check my phone again, Levi had replied saying, "Deal," and I willed the clock to hurry up so I could get out of here.

Finally, after the slowest hour in the entire fucking universe, detention was over, and I could make my escape.

"Where are you rushing off to?" Danny's brows lifted as he took in the way I was shoving everything into my bag as fast as humanly possible.

My brain froze, and I said the first thing that came to mind. "Work."

"I thought you said you didn't have work today?"

"Oh, yeah. I forgot." Blowing out a heavy breath, I forced myself to slow down so he didn't get suspicious. His gaze kept sliding to mine as we walked out, though, and I knew that he could tell something was up.

When we reached the road where we went our separate ways, he stopped, kicking at the kerb. "I know something's up with you."

"There's nothing, Dan."

"Yeah, alright. If you say so." He sighed. "Whatever, I'll see you tomorrow, yeah?"

"Yeah," I said, my stomach twisting with the knowledge

that I was lying to my best mate, and we both knew it. But I couldn't tell him. Not yet.

When I showed up at Levi's house, he wasn't in the media room, so I headed up to his bedroom, finding him sprawled out on his bed in loose grey shorts and a navy T-shirt, playing with his phone. All my guilty thoughts left me as soon as I saw him, and before I even knew what I was doing, I was bounding across the room and launching myself at his bed, throwing myself on top of him.

A startled cry fell from his lips that was instantly swallowed up when my mouth came down on his.

"Hi," he said when he'd rolled us over and pinned me underneath him. "They finally let you escape?"

"They made me miss football training."

"Awww."

I glared up at him. "Fuck you and your fake sympathy." Twisting our bodies, I rolled us back so now I was the one on top. Pinning his wrists down on the bed, I lowered my head and mouthed at his jaw. "Like you've never been in detention."

"I haven't." He stared up at me, all false innocence, so I tugged his lip between my teeth and bit down. A soft moan sounded in his throat, and I forgot all about pretending to be annoyed at him, releasing his lip and sliding my tongue into his mouth. He got his wrists free, and his arms came around me, his hands pulling my T-shirt up my back.

I lifted up from him, helping him rid me of my T-shirt, then slid down his body to his stomach. His cock was hard in his shorts, and I'd promised him a blowjob, but that could wait for now. Pushing his T-shirt up, I left soft bites and kisses all the way up his body, stopping to tug his nipple between my teeth. He gasped, his hips thrusting up.

"Sensitive nipples, huh? I'll have to remember that." Lifting my head, I grinned at him, then lowered my head again. A strangled "fucking hell" came from above me, and his hands dug into my ass while he ground his dick against my thigh. My own cock was hard and aching in my jeans, and when he grabbed a handful of my hair and yanked my head up so he could kiss me, I'd had enough. I pushed away from him, tugging off my jeans and underwear, then pulled down his shorts, exposing his hard length.

I sucked in a sharp breath as I took him in. "You're so—"

"Come up here." His low, rasped command made my cock jump as he stared down at me through lowered lashes with his dark, smoky gaze. Yeah, I wasn't going to say no to that. Crawling up his body, I held myself above him for a few seconds, wanting to prolong the torture, but he was too impatient. He pulled me down, my legs on either side of his.

The first slide of his bare dick against mine was like nothing else. My hips rolled down, and I swallowed his groan in a kiss that quickly turned messy as I moved against him.

The friction of our bodies as we moved together was unbelievably hot. "I never knew this would feel so good," I panted against his ear, getting a hand down between us.

A low moan fell from his throat. "Ash, *fuck*. Me neither." He thrust his dick up as I took us both in my hand, gripping my ass harder and sinking his teeth into my shoulder. A few more thrusts and he was coming between us, covering us both in his release. The feel of his cum all over my dick, his hard body shuddering against mine, and his groans and pants close to my ear sent me straight over the edge with him. My whole body shook as I buried my face in his neck, completely fucking overcome.

Collapsing down on top of him, I tried to get my breath back. His hand came up to stroke through my hair, and he let me lie on him for a minute longer before he prodded at my shoulder.

"You're a dead weight. Get off me."

I rolled off him and onto my back next to him, staring down at my body. "Look at the mess we made."

"Yeah, and I didn't even get my blowjob." He smiled at me.

"Doesn't seem like you're too upset."

"I'm not." Leaning over to kiss me, he rubbed his thumb across my jaw. "I haven't come that hard since…since the last time you made me come."

"Same. My hand's such a poor substitute these days." I stuck my lip out, pouting, and he laughed, tracing his thumb over my lip. When I darted my tongue out to lick it, he inhaled sharply.

"You're too much sometimes."

"What do you mean?"

"You make me hard without even trying. Sometimes you just look at me in a certain way, and I—" Cutting himself off, he shook his head, his cheeks flushed. "You know," he mumbled.

My stomach flipped. "Yeah. I know." I threw my hand over my face. "Same for me."

His mouth pressed against mine in a soft kiss before he drew back. "Come on, let's get cleaned up, and then I'll feed you. Then you owe me a blowjob."

"It's a deal."

Hours later, way after the point I should've left to go home, Levi was sitting in the passenger seat of my car. He'd come out to say goodbye, but we'd been sitting here for well over an hour now, just talking about anything and everything. And kissing. So much kissing, my mouth was getting sore.

It was so fucking good. I'd never known anything like this before, someone who could turn me on so much with just a single look, someone I could spar with who was my match physically, someone who was on the same level as me in every way.

I was really, really into Levi Woodford. And somehow, it seemed that he felt the same way.

NINETEEN
LEVI

There was a rumour, and it wasn't going away. People weren't forgetting about the rivalry, and they wanted retaliation, even though both Asher and I had spread the word it was over. The more time I wanted to spend with Asher, the more apprehensive I grew.

I didn't want anything to happen to him.

"What's up with you? You haven't been yourself lately." Milo threw down the controller, turning to me as the screen announced him as the winner. It was the third game in a row I'd lost, and he was right. I wasn't myself.

Would it hurt to tell him? Not about my feelings for Asher, but about everything else? It was killing me to keep it all inside.

"We need beer for this conversation. Can you get a lift home? Or you can stay over if you want."

He gave me his full attention. "Right. If it's that kind of conversation, I'm ordering pizza, and we're drinking something stronger than beer."

When the pizza turned up and we were on our third beer each, interspersed with shots of some lemon-flavoured spirit he'd dug out from the back of a cupboard in my parents' kitchen, I couldn't hold back anymore.

"There's two things. The first one...you already know."

Pausing in the process of picking the mushrooms off his pizza, because he was one of those weird people who didn't like them, he glanced over at me. "The rivalry?"

"Yeah. You know the rumours aren't dying away. If anything, people are getting worse. They want payback for the gym, and the fact that the fight was a draw..." I trailed off with a shrug, leaning forwards to grab a slice of pepperoni pizza.

He raised a brow. "Don't *you* want payback?"

"What I want is to concentrate on my final year without being distracted by all this shit. If we retaliate, they retaliate. It won't end."

When he finished chewing, he nodded slowly. "You're right. You know...some of the guys on the football team have been saying the same thing. A lot of people are under pressure from their parents, and thinking about the future, you know? They need to do well in their final year, not be distracted by all this other stuff."

"That's exactly it. I've got my provisional acceptance at Southwark University, and if I don't get the grades, I'm not getting in." I washed down my slice of pizza with my beer, then reached for another. "This whole rivalry won't even matter after we finish school."

"I guess all we can do is keep putting out the fires and hope that people get bored of it. We can spread the word with the football team. But are you sure you don't want to put Asher Henderson in his place? Even a bit?"

I wanted to put Asher Henderson in his place. In my bed. Under me, on top of me, whatever he wanted. As long as he was there with me. "We fought, and we drew. I'm done with it now."

Milo grabbed another slice of pizza, dumping the mushrooms on my piece. "Okay. Fair enough. So what's the second thing?"

"It's nothing to do with the first thing"–*lie*–"but it's been playing on my mind." *Truth*. "It's...shit." Placing down the remains of my pizza, I leaned against the back of the sofa, flinging my arm across my face. "I think I'm into men."

There was dead silence. I lowered my hand from my face, watching as Milo's pizza slipped from his grip, falling back into the box while he stared at me in shock. "What, like you're gay?"

"Maybe. Or bi. Or something. I think I've known it for a while...I just... Look, there's someone I like, okay?"

After a minute or two gaping at me, my best friend finally recovered. "There's a guy you like? Who—no, you don't have to tell me. Do you, uh. Is there anything I can do?"

I shook my head. "No. I'm just... I guess I'm sick of keeping it all inside. I needed to tell someone."

There was another moment of silence, and then he gave a brisk nod. "I get it. I'm always here to support you, you know that. And whoever you like, whatever their gender or orientation...that doesn't even matter to me. You're my best friend, and unless you suddenly have a personality transplant or become a serial killer or something, that isn't going to change."

My hands shook as I picked up my pizza again. Telling him...that had taken all of my courage, and to hear that he supported me, fuck. I guess it was all overwhelming. Clearing my throat, I threw him a grateful smile. "I don't know about you, but I need another shot."

"Yeah, me too. It's not every day that your best friend comes out to you. Am I supposed to bake you a cake or something?"

"What the fuck? Where did you get that idea?" I shoved at his shoulder, and he laughed.

"Pinterest, probably. My sister. She shows me all this shit, I don't know. All her mood boards for every bloody thing."

"Yeah, blame her." Smirking, I poured us both another shot. "Seriously, though, thanks."

"You're welcome."

10:30 p.m. Milo had left, and I was straddling the line between tipsy and drunk. I wanted to see Asher, so I texted him. He would've finished work by now.

Me: Can you come here?
Loser: Your house?
Me: Yes. Saturday night and I'm alone and I want to see you
Loser: OMW

While I was waiting for him, I knocked back another shot, then closed my eyes for a second.

"Levi."

My eyes flew open to see Asher grinning down at me. "Ash." I yanked him down onto the sofa, falling into a lying position with him straddling me. My head was spinning, and something hard was digging into my leg. "Is that a knife in your pocket, or are you just pleased to see me?"

A laugh burst from him, and he shoved his hand into his pocket, withdrawing his knife in its sheath, which he threw on the table. "Both, but yeah, it's Ruby." He examined my face intently. "Are you drunk?"

"No. Tipsy."

"Yeah, that's why you're slurring your words."

"You're so sexy." I tugged him closer, kissing whatever part of him I could reach. "I'm so lucky."

He snorted, amused, lifting himself off me. "Come on, drunk boy. Let's go to bed."

We made it up to my bedroom, and he managed to shove me onto my bed without too much trouble. While I'd tipped over to the side of drunk, rather than tipsy, I wasn't so bad that I didn't know what I was doing. More…my inhibitions were lowered.

"If either of us was going to get into this state, I would've put money on it being me, not you." He stretched out on the bed next to me, rubbing his thumb over my cheek. "You haven't shaved. I like it."

"I like you." I shifted closer.

"Mutual." His lips curved upwards. "What's with the drinking, anyway?"

"I told Milo about us. No, not us. Me. Liking men."

"Oh." He stared at me, his thumb still stroking across my jaw. "I get why you were drinking now." Leaning forwards, he brushed a light kiss over my lips. "I'm proud of you. I hope…I hope I'm ready to do the same soon." He inhaled shakily. "As much as it scares the fuck out of me."

"You have to do it in your own time."

"I know." Lifting himself onto his elbow, he studied me again. "We can talk about this more when you're sober. Do you need water or painkillers or anything?"

"No. I'm not that drunk."

"Will you let me drive your car?"

"Nope."

He huffed out a laugh. "Okay, you're not that drunk. But you're drunk enough. You should still drink some water."

Tugging him back down to me, I gave him a soft kiss. "Okay. Can you stay tonight?"

"Yeah, I can stay."

We got ready for bed, and as much as both my dick and his wanted to see some action, he wouldn't let anything happen since I'd been drinking and he hadn't, being way more responsible than I'd ever expected him to be. We ended up with him spooning me, pressing kisses to my shoulder while he stroked up and down my torso, not helping with my dick situation.

"It's torture having you in bed with me when you won't let me do anything about it."

Asher groaned, rolling onto his back. "It's torture for me, too. Next time you invite me over, don't drink. Or drink with me."

When I rolled over to face him, my hand drifted down to his cock tenting the fabric of his underwear, but he pushed my hand away.

"Next time." His eyes met mine, sleepy and heavy-lidded. "Next time, I'm gonna fuck you."

"I've been practising with my fingers, did I say?"

He made an agonised noise in his throat, throwing his hand over his face. "Fucking. Torture. Will you just sleep or something?"

"Some boyfriend you are." I buried my face in the pillow. Sudden tiredness overtook me, and I yawned, closing my eyes.

"Boyfriend? What? Levi..."

But sleep was already claiming me.

TWENTY
ASHER

Did Levi even remember his boyfriend comment, and if he did, had he actually meant it, or was it something he'd said in the heat of the moment but didn't actually mean? Whatever it was, I didn't want to be the one to bring it up. Everything between us had been flipped on its head already. What I did know was that I needed to talk to someone.

There was only one person I could trust to give me their honest advice. Two, really, but telling them both at once wasn't an option. Talking about feelings with Danny...that wasn't something we did.

"I haven't got long before my shift," I told Talia as she handed me a glass of water, ice cubes clinking inside.

Direct as ever, she got straight to the point, sinking onto her bed next to me. "You're keeping a secret from us."

"Yeah." Sipping my water, stalling for time, I stared at her wall of framed retro movie posters. I gritted my teeth, forcing the words from my lips. "I've been seeing Levi."

"You *what*?" She choked on her own water, sending it sloshing out of the sides of her glass, a massive coughing fit taking over her body. Placing my glass down, I rubbed and patted her back until the coughing was under control and she was breathing normally again.

"Bloody hell, Ash," she gasped. "I wasn't expecting that."

I fixed my gaze back on the posters, a lump coming into my throat. Fuck, if she didn't even accept me, what hope did I have with anyone else?

"Hey." A small hand landed on my thigh, just above my knee. "Look at me."

It was an effort to force my head around, blinking away the sudden moisture in my eyes. I'd never felt so vulnerable in my life.

"Oh, Ash." Sliding closer, she put her arms around me, leaning her head on my shoulder. A soft sigh escaped her. "Talk to me. I don't know why I'm surprised, really. I knew you liked him, I just didn't know he felt the same. It really seemed like he hated you, to me."

"You're not...do you...he's a *he*."

Squeezing me tighter, she shook her head. "That doesn't even factor into it, not for me." Drawing back, she met my gaze. "Okay. Being totally honest here. Back when you and me were on and off, I wouldn't have had any clue that you were into guys, but ever since your obsession with Levi started, I...well. I couldn't exactly tell to begin with, but then you became more obsessed, and, I don't know. It seemed obvious to me that you were into him."

"I don't even know if I'm into guys in general or just him." I rubbed my hand across my face. "My head's so messed up. Fuck, T, he's...I really like him. How fucked up is that? He's my enemy."

"It is a bit fucked up, but I guess you're just proving that saying true, about love and hate being two sides of the same coin." She slanted me a curious look. "How did it even happen between you two? When did it start?"

"That night we trashed their gym, I guess. I dunno... we were fighting, and we were both so angry, and then he kissed me because I was going to stab him—"

"You were going to *stab* him? For real?"

"No. Probably not." I grimaced at her disapproving look. "Anyway, he stalked me at work, and then he gave me the phone...and I guess things just happened."

"So you're, what? Boyfriends?"

"I don't know what we are. Maybe. It's fucking hard. It's not like we can tell anyone."

She stared at me, her lips pursed in thought. "You could tell people."

"No way. I can barely get my head around this as it is, and telling people...not just coming out, but the fact that we're rivals—it would put a target on both of our backs. You won't tell anyone, will you? Not even Danny? I don't wanna ask you to hide shit from him, but I'm not ready to talk about it yet."

"I won't. You have my word."

"Thanks. You're the best." I dropped a kiss on her cheek. "Fuck, I think that was the scariest conversation I ever had."

"It'll all work out. I know it. I'm proud of you, Ash. For telling me. For giving whatever this is between you and Levi a chance. For what it's worth, I think you're totally suited to each other."

"Yeah." I grinned. His face flashed through my mind, and my voice turned soft. "Not just because he's hot as fuck. He gets me, you know? I like being around him."

A huge smile spread across her face as she stared at me, wide-eyed. "Wow. You really, really like him, don't you?"

"Yeah. I really do."

My shift was dragging, and I was stuck in the stockroom, breaking up boxes again. The pile of flattened cardboard was growing, but the towering pile of empty boxes didn't seem to be shrinking.

There was a click, and the box I'd been breaking up fell from my hands. The next moment, a hard body was pressed against my back and an arm was snaking around my waist, holding me in a steely grip.

"Slacking off?" Levi's breath skated over my ear, and I smiled, angling my head to the side so he could graze his teeth down my throat.

"You smell good." Dark, woodsy, and completely fucking sexy.

He smiled against my skin. "Just showered. It's my new body wash."

"Mmm. Makes me want to lick you all over."

His nose trailed down my neck. "It just became my new favourite body wash."

"Mine too." I twisted my head to kiss him. "Since you're here, you can help me break up boxes."

"Do I look like your unpaid labour?"

Pulling away from him, I turned to face him, backing him up against the shelves in my favourite position, nose to nose, our breaths mingling as we stared at each other. "Help me out, and I'll help you out." I lightly bit at his lip, pressing my hips into his.

His arms came around me, his hands sliding into the back pockets of my jeans, tugging me closer. "I can agree to those terms."

"But you still won't agree to let me drive your car?"

Levi laughed, shaking his head. "Still no."

"I told Talia about us today."

He stared at me, open-mouthed. "About you and me?"

I nodded before sliding my mouth across his, losing myself in his kiss. When he pulled back to catch his breath, I told him what had happened.

"She won't say anything to anyone. I trust her with my life. I just...you told Milo, and I needed to tell someone how I..." That was enough. I went for his throat, biting and licking at his skin, not enough to leave a mark that he wouldn't be able to explain away, but enough that he'd feel it.

He groaned, his fingers flexing on my ass, but he wasn't distracted. "To tell someone how you what?"

"You know." I mouthed at his jaw, his light stubble scratchy beneath my lips. Sucking in a breath, I dipped my head lower. "How I feel about you."

His hand slid out of my pocket, coming up to cup my jaw. He tugged my head up, forcing me to look at him. Licking his lips, he swallowed hard. "How *do* you feel about me?"

It took everything in me to hold his gaze. Talking about feelings, that wasn't something that came naturally to me. It had been hard enough just discussing what I had done with Talia earlier. But for Levi, I'd try. "I really, really like you." My voice came out all raspy, and I cleared my throat. "I'm pretty fucking obsessed with you, actually."

"Yeah?" he said softly, staring at me with those gorgeous grey eyes. There was a flush to his cheeks. "I'm pretty fucking obsessed with you, too, Asher."

"Yeah?" I had to clear my throat again, trying to dislodge the sudden lump. "Do you...do you wanna come back to mine after I'm done here?"

When we were standing outside my door, I looked at him, with his perfectly mussed hair, designer jeans, and custom trainers, and I wondered what had possessed me to invite him over to my house. There was a reason that most of our time together was spent at his place.

"It's, uh. I know it's not what you're used to," I mumbled as we entered the narrow, dim hallway. The laminate flooring squeaked loudly under my foot, and I couldn't stop my visible wince.

"Fucking hell, Ash," Levi muttered from behind me, yanking me around to face him. He looked almost angry. "I don't care what your house looks like. You could be living in a cave, and it still wouldn't matter to me. I know I can be an entitled, spoiled asshole, but this?" Waving a hand in the air, he stared at me. "I. Don't. Care."

"Oh. Alright."

He sighed, tugging me into his arms. "I'm sorry if I ever made you feel less. You're not... Look. If you don't realise just how lucky I am to have you, then you need your head examined."

There wasn't even anything I could say to that. I felt too fucking raw, and I needed space. Pulling out of his grip, I started off down the hallway and up the narrow staircase to the tiny landing. Behind me, I heard his heavy tread as he followed me up the stairs, and I pushed open my bedroom door, leaving it wide open to let him in. After kicking off my trainers, I placed my palms on my dresser, facing away from Levi, breathing in and out deeply to try and get myself under control.

"I know what you need." His voice was sure from behind me. "Just like you know what I need." Then he jumped me, slamming me into my dresser, knocking the breath from my lungs.

Yes. My pulse jumped as I threw him off me, making him stumble backwards. There wasn't far he could go— my bedroom was small, and my double bed took up the majority of the floor space. He crashed onto my bed, and I followed him, pinning him down in a wrestling hold that held him immobile.

"Think you can get the better of me, Seven?" I sat up, straddling him, and he grinned up at me. His eyes darkened as I tugged my polo shirt off, baring my torso to him.

"Your body," he breathed, running his hand over the bumps of my abs. I flexed them under his touch, clamping down on my lip as he stroked his fingers down my happy trail and onto the bulge in my jeans.

The next second, I was on my back, staring at him in shock as his body weight held me in place.

"You shouldn't let yourself get so distracted, *Ten*." Mimicking my move, he pushed himself up and dragged his T-shirt over his head. I ran my hands over his abs, but he didn't let himself get distracted, not like I had.

Time to try a different trick. I licked my lips, holding his gaze, while I reached out with my hand, feeling around until I hit my bedside table. It took a bit of manoeuvring, but I eventually managed to get the drawer open, and my hand closed around the small bottle. All the while, he tracked me with his hot, hungry gaze.

My cock ached for him.

"Look what I have."

Finally, his attention was drawn to what I held in my hand. "Is that—"

I took my chance and struck, bucking him off my body and rolling us both over. He flipped me, and then I flipped him. He sank his teeth into my shoulder, and then I sank mine into his throat.

But when I managed to get my hand down between us, undoing his jeans and yanking them down before he even had a chance to react, it was game over.

He lay on his back, breathing hard as I rid him of his underwear, watching me through blown pupils. "*Asher*." He groaned low in his throat as my hand wrapped around his cock. "You win. Fuck. I want you so badly."

I shifted up his body to lie next to him with my thigh slung across his leg, pumping him in a slow, lazy movement. "How do you want me? Do you wanna fuck me? Or do you want me to fuck you?" I gave his cock one last, long stroke, then let my hand drift lower, over his balls, and lower still, until my finger was ghosting over his hole.

"*Yes*. Don't stop."

His chest rose and fell in sharp movements as he watched me uncap the small bottle of lube that I'd swiped from work, putting it through the till myself to avoid unwanted questions. His body was flushed from his face right down to his hard cock, the tip wet with precum, and he looked so fucking gorgeous that my breath caught in my throat, my heart pounding as I raked my gaze over every inch of him.

"You. You are a fucking work of art."

He gave me a smile that was almost shy, his gaze flicking from my eyes to my fingers. His tongue darted out again to wet his lips, and he swallowed thickly. "*Please.*"

"Uh. Do you want to lie on your stomach?"

In reply, he manoeuvred himself onto his front, and I took a second just to drink his body in from this angle. Fuck. I had to touch him. Leaning over him, I ran my hands down the lean muscles of his back, following the path of my hands with my mouth, kissing and licking over his skin.

"Tell me if I hurt you. I'm gonna go as slow as I can."

With a soft sound of agreement, he buried his face in the pillow, widening his legs to give me better access. I drizzled the lube over my fingers and between his ass cheeks. Sucking in a shaky breath, I dragged my finger down, circling over the rim of his hole, before I dared to push it in. He tensed, and I stroked my other hand over his ass.

"It's gonna feel so good when I'm inside you. Filling you up with my cock."

Fuck, I never spoke like this, but if his muffled groans were anything to go by, I needed to keep it up. His hips thrust shallowly into the mattress as I eased it further in, feeling him contract around me, hot and tight, until my finger was buried inside his body.

"Fuck, baby. I'm all the way in. How does it feel?"

He moaned, his head rolling to the side. "It burned, then you…you touched me."

"Your prostate? You like that?" I drew my finger back a bit until I found the spot I was looking for. I pressed down lightly, and his hips bucked.

"*Fuck*. Yeah, that."

Stroking across the sensitive area, I eased a second finger in at the same time, circling it around, opening him up for me. All my research was paying dividends, based on his reaction.

"Two fingers now. My dick's so hard for you." I curled my body over his, kissing up the side of his jaw and up to his ear, where I lightly bit down. "Do you think you can take another?"

"Yeah." His voice was wrecked. "You don't even know…"

"You're gonna do this to me next time."

He moaned, contracting around my fingers again. I shifted back, adding some more lube before I carefully pushed a third finger in. He was so fucking tight, and I took my time opening him up until he was begging me to fuck him.

"I can't take any more. Fuck me, *please*." His fingers white-knuckled the bedsheets as he turned his head to meet my gaze, his pupils so dilated that there was barely any silver visible, just the smoky ring around the edge.

I swallowed hard.

"Okay."

TWENTY-ONE
LEVI

When he'd slowly withdrawn his fingers, I felt... empty. I needed him inside me, to push me over the edge I'd been riding while he drove me completely insane with his fingers. His head dipped to my ear. "I wanna fuck you so hard, but not for our first time. Today, we're gonna take it slow. How do you want to do this?"

A vivid image flashed through my brain—Asher, pounding hard, his hips snapping against me as I watched him lose control.

"No. I want you to fuck me hard." I didn't even recognise my voice. He'd wrecked me already, and he hadn't even got his dick in my ass yet. "Like this." Shifting onto my back, I stared up at him.

"Okay." He swallowed, his throat working, his gaze darkening as I took my cock in my hand, palming the length. "Yeah."

Leaning forwards, he placed a soft kiss to my lips before taking hold of the pillow that was next to my head. Sliding it under me, he moved forwards, his hands coming down under my thighs.

"Put your legs up over my shoulders."

I lifted my legs to his shoulders, and as I did, there was a click as he unsnapped the cap of the lube again, followed by the rip of a condom packet opening and then a cool slippery sensation as he coated both me and him with the lube. I felt the head of his cock at my hole, then a pressure, and he was pushing inside me, teeth clamped down on his lip, his lashes lowered as he stared down at his dick entering me.

Even with the lube and the stretching he'd done, it burned, but I wanted more. Wanted him to fill me. I continued palming my cock, taking deep, steady breaths, until his thick length was all the way inside me.

I was so fucking full.

We both stilled, sharing panted breaths, and his eyes locked on mine. Then, he moved, dragging his dick in a slow, torturous pace until he was almost all the way out.

I licked my lips slowly, deliberately, as I held his gaze, sliding my hand down my cock.

"Fuck me, Asher. Hard."

His eyes flashed with pure lust, and his lips curved into a wild, savage grin. "Hold on, baby." He thrust his hips once, his cock rubbing over that spot inside me that felt so fucking good, I jerked upwards with a hoarse cry.

"Fuck, *there*."

"Yeah, you like that?" He thrust again, and again, and again, nailing my prostate and sending me spiralling. My breath caught in my throat, overwhelmed by the sensations of his powerful body curled over mine, his hard length filling me up, and my own hand pumping my erection, slippery with precum.

As he pounded in and out of me, whatever discomfort I'd felt faded into nothing, replaced by a pleasure so fucking intense that I knew I wasn't going to last any longer. My vision blurred as my muscles tightened, my balls drawing up and my dick throbbing in my hand, hot ropes of cum covering my torso.

He groaned, pounding me even harder as I came, and then his cock was pulsing inside me, spilling his release into the condom. Sweat dripped from his head onto me, his chest rising and falling rapidly as he gasped for breath, finally collapsing on top of me, uncaring of the mess.

Lowering my legs, I wound my arms around his shaking body. As we lay there, catching our breaths, I knew right then that I was completely fucked. No one else would ever compare to Asher Henderson.

"Ash?"

"Yeah?" He turned his head to face mine, sprawled out on his stomach next to me. We'd cleaned up and then ended up back in his bed, even though I'd told him I was going to go home an hour earlier.

"Last week...when I'd been drinking, I said something."

His gaze turned wary. "Uh-huh."

I placed my palm on his warm back, tracing circles there. "I called you my boyfriend."

"I remember." Both his face and voice were inscrutable, and I had no idea what he was thinking, but I pushed through. We both needed to know where we stood.

"Did—was that okay with you?" Clearing my throat, I added, "Because I want that."

Asher stared at me for a long moment, his gaze going so soft that I needed to kiss him more than I needed to take my next breath. I moved closer, my lips coming down on his. He opened up to me, rolling to his side, his mouth a hot, slow slide against mine.

"Yeah, that was okay," he rasped against my lips. "I want that, too." Pulling his head back to meet my gaze, he traced his thumb across my lips, a harsh breath escaping him when I bit down lightly.

"It still blows my mind. That out of everyone in the world, I ended up with you." A smile tugged at my lips. "You attacked me, threatened me with a knife, trashed my school, fought me in the bowl...what else am I forgetting?"

"All the stuff on the football pitch. Uh...I broke into your house once or twice. Or more." He grinned unapologetically. "You gave it back to me just as good, though."

"Yep. I did."

"Sounds like we're perfect for each other." His mouth covered mine, sucking my bottom lip between his before releasing.

"We are." My smile dropped as I ran my hand up his arm, across his shoulder, to thread through his messy hair. "I know that I've done plenty of shit to you that I should regret, but I can't totally regret it, because we probably wouldn't be here right now."

"Same. If you're feeling any regrets, you know how you could make it up to me?"

"If your suggestion is that I let you drive my car, the answer is no."

He nipped at my jaw. "I know I'll wear you down one of these days."

"If you say so." I kissed him again before reluctantly

breaking away with a heavy sigh. "There was something else I wanted to talk to you about."

"The rivalry." His tone turned grim.

"I know you say you can handle it, but this isn't dying down. As much as I've tried to put out the fires, and so has Milo and even some of the football team, there are still people that want Highnam to pay. They're frustrated that we're not acting against you anymore, and they're not going to be happy until they've done something about it. That means you're a prime target, and it's killing me worrying about you."

"I know they want payback." He tugged me into his arms. "I'll be careful, and I'm gonna do everything I can to make sure that if anyone tries anything, Highnam doesn't react in any way. This started with us; it has to end with us."

Although his words were reassuring, I couldn't stop the unease that was a constant presence in my mind.

If anyone tried to fuck with my boyfriend, they'd regret it.

TWENTY-TWO
ASHER

Exiting the shop with a wave to Selina, I jogged across the street, a box of microwave popcorn and a bag of Haribo in my hand. I hadn't been working today, but it was the closest place to my house, and I needed snacks for meeting up with Levi. He was at football training, but by the time he got home, I'd have made myself comfortable in his house. As much as he complained about the fact that I was always breaking in and helping myself to his stuff, I knew he loved it. I grinned to myself, already anticipating his huge rainfall showerhead and that body wash I was getting a bit addicted to. I might not have loads of spare cash to flash around, but I could guarantee that my boyfriend would rather be surprised by me waiting for him naked in his shower than some expensive, meaningless shit. Somehow, he was just as into me as I was into him, despite the odds, despite everything that had gone down between us.

We were into December now, and even though it was still early, it was dark, and the alleyway was wreathed in shadows. Picking up the pace, I headed for the streetlight shining at the far end, taking care with my movements since the ground was slippery from the heavy rain that had been falling for most of the day, although it had let up around an hour ago. I glanced down at my feet every now and then to make sure I didn't step on any broken glass in the darkness. It was a lottery of what you might find down here. Come to think of it, broken glass was probably the least of my worries.

There was a sound behind me like a baseball bat makes whistling through the air, and I spun, ducking just in time to avoid the large piece of wood swinging at my head.

There was no time to think, only to react, my body working on instinct, dodging my assailant.

Fuck. There were two more behind them. No, three.

Time to cut my losses.

One thing you learned living round here—if a gang jumped you and you didn't have backup, you didn't hang around. You got the fuck out of there. Even my knife was no use against a whole group of people.

With that in the back of my mind, I made for the exit of the alleyway, but I was yanked back by my hoodie. Losing my balance on the rain-slicked surface, I found myself falling backwards, landing on the wet, cracked concrete with a thud. The popcorn and Haribo were lost, forgotten as all the air was knocked out of my lungs, and I gasped for breath.

I was down, but not out. I just had to create an opening so I could get out of there. Rolling away from the booted foot coming at me, I swiped one of my assailant's legs from under me, sending them crashing to the ground. Before I had a chance to incapacitate them, there was the sound of running footsteps, and another figure appeared, lunging at me, knocking me back to the ground. Someone else's body weight joined the first, pinning my legs down, while from above me there were jeers and shouts.

Five against one?

I didn't ever really stand a chance.

When my energy was spent, they mashed my face into the cold, dirty ground, kicking and punching my body. I remained silent, refusing to give them the satisfaction of hearing my voice, hunching over and curling into myself, absorbing the blows, until all I saw was black.

There were flashes after that.

Hands dragging me along, fingers digging into my arms. Another kick. Another blow to my back. Shocks of pain radiating through my entire body. The vibrations of a car engine. Low voices muttering about payback being served.

Everything hurt too much for me to make sense of any of it.

We rounded a corner and my head smacked into the side of the car, ricocheting off the glass. Stars exploded behind my eyelids at the sudden burst of pain.

Mocking laughter sounded, before the darkness descended again.

TWENTY-THREE
LEVI

We were heading off the floodlit football pitch when there was a commotion at the far end of the field. I exchanged glances with Milo.

"What the fuck's going on over there?"

"I'll check it out." Carl jogged off while I stood with Milo, staring as a group of figures came into view, accompanied by shouts.

"Levi!" Carl's voice cut through the noise, and I ran.

At first, I couldn't make sense of what I was seeing. There was a group of five people—three guys from our school year and two from the year below, dragging someone between them. They dropped the person when I got close, and that was when I got my first proper look, the floodlights throwing everything into sharp relief.

A choked cry tore from my lips, and I fell to my knees next to Asher's prone body, cradling his head in my hands. He was soaked through, covered in mud, his clothes torn and his face bruised and battered. Cuts bled from his swelling lip and his cheek, and one of his eyes was swollen shut.

"Asher. Oh, fuck. *Asher*." Brushing his wet hair away from his face, I curled over him, my voice dropping to a panicked whisper. "Baby, wake up." I didn't even realise I was crying until I felt the tears on my cheeks, hot against the freezing winter air.

He gave a deep, shuddering gasp, his eye that wasn't swollen opening a slit. "L-Levi?"

The relief of hearing his voice was instantaneous, and with it came a rage so powerful that I knew I would tear apart the world for him.

Looking up, I saw all eyes on me with Asher, jaws dropped, alternating disbelief and horror written all over everyone's faces. Ignoring the tears that were still tracking down my cheeks, I let the rage bleed through my voice, into my eyes, directing it at the five hooded guys.

"Carl. Go and check if the coach has left. The rest of you, take these five into the changing rooms. I'll be there in a minute. Milo, stay here."

Because the football team respected me and were used to following orders, and probably because they were in shock, they obeyed me despite throwing me questioning looks, grabbing the guys and making off with them in the direction of the gym.

Milo crouched down next to me. "What do you need me to do?"

"I need to get hold of Asher's friend Danny. We need to get Asher out of here. We don't know if those guys acted alone, and I need him safe."

"Okay. Do you have—"

"Pock...pocket," Asher rasped.

"I've got it." I eased his phone out of his pocket. "Surprised they didn't take this," I muttered to Milo as he helped me to lay Asher flat on the ground. It had a thumbprint lock, so I gently pressed it to Asher's thumb and then handed the phone to Milo to make the call.

"He's the one, isn't he?" A minute or two later, Milo crouched down next to me again, where I was carefully checking Asher for any injuries.

"Yeah. He's the one." My voice cracked. "Fuck, I don't think I can confront those guys right now. I'm scared of what I might do to them."

Milo placed a reassuring hand to my shoulder. "Don't do anything you'll regret, but remember that you're not in this alone. You're going to have to give the boys an explanation for all this, but they've got your back."

But who had Asher's?

Seating myself again so his head was in my lap, I stroked over his face. "Ash, can you tell me where it hurts? I need to make sure we don't need to take you to A&E or anything."

"S'okay. Just...punches...kicks. I protected...my ribs."

I didn't even know what to say. It hurt so much to look at him, to see his beautiful face damaged by something that I should've anticipated and stopped before it happened. To know he was in this state because of something I'd had a hand in, even if only indirectly. I'd lit the match, fanned the flames, and even though I'd stepped back, I was now having to watch it burn.

"I'm so fucking sorry." I curled over him, placing a careful, soft kiss to the tip of his nose, which miraculously didn't seem to be broken.

"Not...not your fault." His voice was steadier, less raspy

than it had been. "Not your fault," he repeated.

"Asher!" There was a shout from the edge of the pitch, and Danny came at us at a run. He dropped to the ground next to us. "What the *fuck* happened?"

Asher groaned. "They jumped me...five of them."

"They're going to fucking pay," I ground out, and Danny's gaze flew to mine, seemingly realising for the first time that I had Asher's head in my lap, and my fingers were stroking through his hair.

"This explains *so* much," he muttered under his breath. "Is he okay to be moved?" he said more loudly.

"Just bruises. They didn't even take Ruby. Fu...fucking amateurs." Behind the swelling, I saw the very corner of Asher's mouth twitch, and I traced my thumb over the spot with the barest hint of a touch.

"Okay, I don't wanna be the one to say this, but I will. Forgetting Asher's state for a minute, is anyone else finding it really fucking weird that his arch-enemy is cosying up to him?" Danny glanced over at Milo, who gave me a shrug, then nodded at him with a wry smile.

"Thought so. Okay, time to get you home, Ash. Can one of you help me get him to the car?" He looked between me and Milo.

Milo turned to me, his tone firm. "I'll make sure he makes it to the car safely. You need to get inside and..." He paused. "Do whatever you need to do. I'll join you after."

"Okay." I really, really didn't want to leave Asher, but he needed to get away from here, and I needed to make someone pay for what they'd done to him. Together, the three of us got him to his feet, and supported by Danny and Milo, he managed to stand.

Uncaring of what they both thought, I leaned forwards,

pressing a kiss to the skin just beneath Asher's ear. "I'll come and find you after."

He huffed out a soft breath. "Don't do anything stupid."

"I'll try not to."

In the gym, the five boys were seated on the benches, the football team standing around them, leaning against the lockers and the walls. Everyone looked up when I entered.

Some of my rage had been left back on the field with the knowledge that Asher's injuries were only superficial, but enough was enough. This ended, right here, right now.

"Most of you probably have questions about my reaction towards what went down out there," I began, thumbing towards the door. "First of all, every single person here should know by now that we'd agreed not to continue this rivalry. There's no excuse—the word's been spreading around the school for long enough. My fight in the bowl with Asher was the end of it."

There were several nods from some of the football team, but the five on the bench stared at me sullenly, mistrust in their eyes.

"I know that wasn't enough for everyone. I know some of you wanted payback. But you need to remember, we started it first. *We* were the ones to trash their gym, and they were only responding to what we'd already done. If we struck back, when would it end? They'd hit us back, and it would go on, and on, and on. Do any of you want your final year as a student to be like this? I certainly fucking don't. A couple of pranks are one thing, but this is getting out of hand."

More nods and murmurs of agreement, and I relaxed

slightly. Milo entered the changing room at that point, giving me a small, reassuring smile before heading over to stand against the wall with our teammates.

"As for what happened tonight." My voice lowered, the threat implicit in my tone. "Someone had better start talking, *right fucking now*."

"We thought you'd be pleased that we were bringing you your enemy on a plate," Declan eventually spoke up. I was surprised and honestly fucking angry that he'd been involved—he was one of the school prefects, and I'd never known him to get his hands dirty before.

"It was his idea!" One of the younger guys, Keegan, pointed at the guy at the end of the row. "He said we needed to make them pay."

"We were meant to be videoing it and uploading the footage," his friend muttered, clearly deciding that it was safer to confess than to remain silent. "I videoed it, but I didn't upload it anywhere, I promise."

"Give me your phone." I stalked up to him, and with a shaking hand, he passed it to me.

When the video started playing, I had to look away after a few seconds. I couldn't watch my boyfriend being beaten by these guys. It was too much. Instead, I passed the phone around the team, making sure they'd all seen it. The atmosphere in the room grew sombre as the video played, evidence of the brutal attack unleashed on Asher. They'd all seen him lying there on the field, too, and it was clear that the sight of him had shaken us all.

When the phone had been handed to the last person, and the footage had been forwarded to Milo's phone, then deleted from the source, I cleared my throat. Speaking through gritted teeth, with my fists clenched tightly to hide my shaking hands, I forced my feelings to one side so I could get through this. "Five against one is *not* payback. No one will ever respect you for that. It's not a fair fight—all it does is make you look like a pack of thugs who took on one innocent man who was defenceless and alone. Do you know how completely fucking stupid you were? Just from the few seconds I saw, I could make out at least three of your faces. If this footage actually gets out anywhere, you'll be expelled from Alstone High. I'm sure that would go down well with your parents. Oh, and you can look forward to an arrest for assault and most likely ABH charges."

Now they weren't looking at me with anger and resentment. There was panic written all over their faces.

"Yeah. Think about that." I took the time to look at each one of their faces. "As for my reaction to your unforgivable stunt back outside. That guy you jumped, Asher Henderson?" I paused. I couldn't out him or our relationship without his permission, so I settled on a half-truth. "Yes, we were rivals. But he's a friend of mine now. A good friend. I look out for my friends, and if someone hurts one of them, well…" A savage grin twisted across my lips. "They have to pay."

"*Please*, no." Keegan spoke up again, his voice shaking.

Milo stepped up next to me, flashing me a warning look. "Fortunately for you, we're feeling generous. In the showers. Now."

The five of them got up without another word and headed into the shower room, the door swinging shut behind them. When they were safely out of earshot, I addressed the rest of the team. "Does anyone else have any questions for me?"

"Are you seriously friends with Asher Henderson?" Carl

finally said, echoing what everyone else was wondering, going by the curious eyes on me. "You weren't just saying it?"

"Yeah, we're friends." I gave him a crooked smile. "He's alright when he's not being an asshole."

"I always thought he seemed alright," one of my other teammates offered, and that was that. They accepted my words, even though I knew that most, if not all of them, would have their suspicions about the true nature of mine and Asher's relationship. In particular, the trio of teammates that had run into both me and Asher at the cinema, who were now giving each other sideways glances.

"If we want this shit to stop here, we can't punish the guys too badly," Carl spoke up again to murmurs of assent. "As much as you probably want to fuck them up after what they did, the reminder of what would happen if the footage gets out should be enough of a deterrent to stop them trying anything else, and I think for now—"

"I need them to hurt physically, after what they did to Asher," I growled, the anger returning.

"In that case, how about we push them in the showers—"

"—fully clothed, then we can—"

"—turn the showers on—"

"—nah, we don't wanna get wet. We should act quickly—"

"—don't wanna get wet? Scared of a bit of water?"

"—get a punch in before they know what's coming. Hit them where it hurts. A reminder—"

"—then let them know if word gets out about any of this, their lives won't be worth living."

As my teammates took matters into their own hands, I stood back, confident in the knowledge that justice would be served. I had other priorities. Number one on the list: I needed to see my boyfriend and make sure he was okay.

TWENTY-FOUR
LEVI

"He's asleep. And so's his mum, so don't go waking them up." Danny faced me on the doorstep of Asher's house, his face wary.

"Okay. I just want to see him."

He rolled his eyes at me. "Yeah, I guessed that." Stepping closer, he lowered his voice. "He hasn't told me anything about you, but I have eyes, and...yeah. I can put two and two together."

"I—"

"Don't tell me anything. If he wants to share, it can come from him."

I eyed him cautiously. "For what it's worth, I'm sorry for what happened tonight. It's been taken care of, and it won't happen again."

His wary expression finally disappeared, and he sighed, shaking his head. "Ash might not have said anything about whatever's going on between you two, but he made it clear that I wasn't allowed to blame you." Moving aside to let me in the front door, he added, "Even though I want to."

"Yeah. That makes two of us." I stepped past him, over the threshold, and he moved onto the path leading back to the road. When he reached the pavement, he turned back to me.

"We've patched each other up enough after fights at the bowl. Everything's superficial—there's nothing that you need to be worrying about. He's gonna be fine."

I acknowledged his words with a nod, then took the final step into Asher's house and closed the door behind me.

When I entered his bedroom, he was lying on his back, illuminated by the dim glow of the lamp on his bedside table. A bag of frozen peas was propped half on his pillow, half on his face, and there was a small adhesive Steri-Strip across the cut on his cheek.

A lump came into my throat, seeing him so battered. Quietly shutting the door behind me, I removed my shoes and crossed over to his bed. I'd had the world's quickest shower and changed after everything that had happened, not wanting to show up damp and muddy, and I was glad of it now as I lay down on his clean bedcovers, resting my head on the pillow next to his. I didn't want to wake him, but I had to touch him. Carefully reaching out for his hand, I threaded my fingers between his.

Then I closed my eyes, and somehow, sleep came.

"Hi."

I blinked my eyes open to see Asher facing me, a small smile pulling at his lips.

"How...how are you feeling?" I croaked, rubbing at my

eyes.

"Like I went ten rounds with the current champion of the bowl."

I returned his smile. "That's me."

"I know." As he watched me, my gaze tracked over him, cataloguing his injuries. The bruises were darkening, changing colour and looking worse than they had yesterday, but I knew that was part of the healing process. The swelling over his eye had gone down significantly, although it was still swollen, turning an angry purple. His lip swelling had reduced, too, and now it had, I could see that the cut there was only small, not anything that would've needed stitches.

Shifting closer, I stroked my thumb across his cheekbone. "I wish I'd been here to take care of you."

He reached down for my hand, sliding his fingers between mine. "I know you couldn't be, and I had Danny to help. Anyway, you're here now."

"I'm not going anywhere, Asher."

Squeezing my hand, he blinked, sudden moisture appearing in his eyes. I swallowed hard to dislodge the lump that had appeared in my throat, and I leaned forwards to place a soft kiss to his lips. When they trembled underneath my touch, I couldn't fucking breathe. All I could do was wrap him carefully in my arms, holding him while he buried his face in my shoulder.

A while later, when I'd been tracing feather-light patterns on his back and placing kisses to his hair, he raised his head. His gorgeous brown eyes were still glassy, his thick lashes shiny and wet, but the soft smile he gave me was genuine. It widened to a grin when he said, "Let's check out my war wounds. I'm betting my back and legs look the worst."

With that, he rolled away from me with a grunt of pain, swinging himself off the bed and tugging his T-shirt over his head, then tugged down his sweatpants. A gasp fell from my lips as I took in the mass of purpling bruises over his body. "Fucking hell, they really went at you." Anger burned through me once more, and I knew that if I'd seen his body in this state yesterday, there was no way that I would've been able to satisfy myself with giving those guys just one punch.

"I've had worse." He shrugged, shooting me another grin. "Maybe not all at once. It hurts, but it's only bruises. Nothing's broken."

Pushing myself up to a seated position, I shook my head at his blasé tone. "You're taking this well."

Sinking back down onto the bed, he glanced over at me. "Yeah. Well. It could've been worse. A lot worse. And it's over now, isn't it? Knowing you and how you probably acted, they won't dare to do anything else. Am I right?"

I spotted a tube of arnica cream over on his chest of drawers. "Lie down and I'll put some of that cream on your bruises." Climbing off the bed, I grabbed the tube as he lowered himself to his stomach. "You're right." As I spread the cream across his bruises, I told him what had happened.

"See. No longer a problem. Now all I have to worry about is being jumped by actual gangs. With knives." He tilted his head back to look up at me, his eyes dancing with amusement.

"That's not even funny." I put the cap back on the tube and then leaned over him to press a kiss to the back of his neck. Climbing off him, I replaced the tube on the dresser.

"Want some breakfast?" Hesitation entered his tone. "You can meet my mum if you want?"

My stomach flipped. "Yes to both. How do you want me

to play this? Your friend who happened to have a sleepover?"

"Uh." He pulled himself upright, wincing slightly. "I wouldn't mind introducing you as my...uh. My boyfriend." His fingers played with his duvet as he stared down at his hands. "But I'm good with telling her we're friends," he added in a rush.

"Fuck it. If you want to tell her, let's tell her. But only if I can tell my parents."

His instant smile was wide and bright. "Deal."

When he was dressed again and I'd spent too long messing with my hair in front of the mirror, to which Asher, the hypocrite with the messiest hair in the entire world, teased me endlessly about, we made our way downstairs and into the small kitchen.

"Mum." Asher cleared his throat.

The dark-haired woman standing at the countertop spun around.

"Asher! What happened to you?" It didn't seem like she'd even noticed me, her tired eyes taking in my boyfriend's face. It was a good thing that the rest of his bruises were currently covered by tracksuit bottoms and a hoodie.

"Got jumped. I didn't see who they were." His gaze flicked to mine as he hugged her to him. "I'm fine. It looks worse than it is."

She drew back, taking his face in her hands, examining it from every angle. Finally satisfied, she released her grip, giving a short nod. "You'll live." Returning to the counter where she'd been making a cup of tea, she fished the bag out of the cup, adding a large splash of milk. After giving it a quick stir, she turned back around to face us. "Aren't you going to introduce me to your friend?"

He sucked in a sharp breath. "Yeah. Mum, this is Levi

Woodford. My...my boyfriend."

Her eyebrows shot up to her hairline, and she clapped a hand over her mouth. "But I thought you liked girls?" she said when she eventually recovered, her confused gaze bouncing between us.

"Yeah. Well. I like him, too." Shifting on his feet, he stared at her, wide-eyed and apprehensive.

She pinched her brow, sighing heavily, then turned to address me. "Levi. Could I have a word with my son in private, please?"

I glanced over at him, and he nodded. Fuck. I didn't want to leave him. I wanted to kiss that anxious expression from his face and reassure him that I wasn't going anywhere. But I didn't. Brushing my fingers over the back of his hand, I left them to it, making my way back upstairs to his bedroom. Picking up my phone to give me something to do, I waited.

When I heard Asher's footsteps on the stairs, I threw my phone down, launching myself off the bed and over to the door. He sighed when he saw me, sliding his arms around me and lowering his head to rest on my shoulder.

"She's going to be okay with it. I think. I hope." Lifting his head, he gave me an uncertain smile, his eyes wide and troubled. "She's not homophobic or anything. I think? I guess it's...it has to be a shock, you know? She's only ever seen me with girls, and, yeah. I mean, obviously I wasn't interested in any guys until you."

I kissed the side of his face, trying to reassure him. "Yeah. I'm proud of you, and I'm here for you whatever happens. You know that, right?"

"I know." His hands stroked down my back. "So that's one down, five million to go."

"Are we telling everyone, then?"

"Do you want to?" He studied me. "I'm...really fucking scared, actually, but I dunno...I can always introduce Ruby to anyone that has a problem with us."

I narrowed my eyes at him.

"Joking! Don't look at me that way. I wouldn't cut them." He coughed out a noise that sounded suspiciously like "much."

"I'm scared, too. But our best friends know now, don't they? I'm sure the rest of the AHS football team have probably worked it out, too, seeing how they saw me crying over you yesterday."

"Baby." He tightened his grip on me, his voice soft. "I thought I hallucinated that."

"Yeah, well, you didn't," I muttered, dropping my head to his shoulder. "It was the worst day of my life."

"It didn't rate in my top ten, either. But it won't happen again. We'll make sure of it."

"Yeah. We will."

TWENTY-FIVE
ASHER

"Alright?" I swung the front door open, letting Danny inside. His mouth was set in a flat line and his eyes were hard. Fuck. He was definitely pissed off with me.

When we reached my bedroom, the two of us settled on my bed, backs against the wall and game controllers in hand, just like we'd been doing for years. He still hadn't said anything, so I pointedly stared at him until he gave in, turning to face me with a huge, exaggerated sigh. Some of the hardness faded from his gaze as he eyed me.

"You look better than you did two days ago."

"Yeah." The swelling on my face was minimal now, and the bruises were mostly on my body. I had a black eye, but that had happened enough that it wasn't anything unusual for me. "Dan. I know you're angry with me."

"You think?" he finally snapped. "I'm supposed to be your best mate, and I find out by chance that you've been having this whole secret relationship behind my back. It's not even the fact that it's Levi—zero fucking surprise there, mate, once I'd thought about it—it was the fact that you hid it from me. If you hadn't been beaten up, would you even have told me? Would you still be lying to me right now?"

All I could do now was give him the truth and hope he'd understand. "Honestly? Maybe." I tipped my head back against the wall, closing my eyes. "I always planned to tell you, but...fuck, it's been a lot to get my head around. You have to understand. This whole thing came out of fucking nowhere. You know how much I hated him. I've had to deal with the fact that not only am I into a man, something that has never happened once in my entire life, but of all the men it could possibly be, it's Levi fucking Woodford, my mortal enemy. Wouldn't that mess your head up if it was you?" Opening my eyes again, I met his gaze. "There's no manual for dealing with this shit. Coming out to you...we're best mates, but I didn't...I didn't know how you'd take it. My own mum's having some, uh, problems coming to terms with it, and she gave birth to me."

He rubbed his hand over his face, the anger leaving his tone. "Yeah. Okay. I get what you're saying." Picking up his controller, he tapped the button that turned on the console. "I didn't mean that you had to tell me that. It was the hiding shit from me that I had a problem with. We always tell each other everything, so, yeah. It hurt me. But just so we're clear, I don't care if you're gay, straight, Levi-sexual, whatever. I think your taste in men is completely fucking abysmal, but—"

I shoved at him, making him lose his balance, and he fell sideways onto the bed, laughing.

We were going to be alright.

"I know you told Talia," he said a bit later, when we'd

progressed from playing games to snacking on Doritos while we watched Netflix.

Fuck.

He must've correctly read the guilt in my expression, because he shook his head. "I went over to hers after I'd left you, when Levi showed up, and she admitted that she knew and you'd asked her to keep it from me. I don't blame her, I was just…hurt. And angry. With you, not her."

At least he hadn't blamed her. They were good together, and if I'd inadvertently fucked anything up between them, I wouldn't have been able to forgive myself. But I hated that I'd hurt my best mate. "Yeah, I know. I'm sorry, Dan."

"It's alright. You don't need to apologise. Like I said, it was the fact that you'd hidden shit from me. You shouldn't have to come out before you're ready."

"Yeah." I scrubbed my hand across my face. "Now I have to go through all this with everyone else. I don't wanna hide it anymore, and now you know, and probably the entire AHS football team does as well, I need to prepare for whatever happens at school."

"Ash." A grin spread across his lips as he shook his head at me. "I think you're underestimating your power. Half the people at school love you because of your football skills… or because they wanna fuck you, I guess." He muttered "No accounting for taste" under his breath, then laughed at my mock glare. "Whatever, you're popular and you know it. And the other half are scared of you because of your fighting skills. They still talk about the time you took down Matt Sims, and that was, what? Three years ago? You're a fucking legend."

"Awww, mate. That's the nicest thing you've ever said to me." Returning his grin, I added, "Don't forget your reputation, either."

"Oh, yeah. I'm just as much of a legend as you. They should put up a plaque in our honour when we leave school." He grabbed a handful of Doritos, smirking at me.

"They should."

"Seriously, though, I've got your back. And Talia has a plan for the whole rivalry thing."

I raised a brow. "What's the plan?"

"She'll tell you when she gets here."

When Talia showed up, she lowered herself gracefully into my desk chair. There was a smile on her face, but when she took in the state of my face, her smile dropped. "Okay. This has to end now." Rising from the chair, she examined me more closely. "If you look like this two days after what happened, I can't even imagine how bad you looked at the time."

"Bad." Danny climbed off the bed to kiss her. "Hi."

Her smile returned. "Hi." She moved to sit on the end of my bed, facing me with Danny next to her. "I have a couple of ideas for how we can draw a line under everything. I'm neutral, and let's face it, the best at planning out of the three of us."

Danny and I looked at each other and shrugged. It was true.

Talia tapped out something on her phone, then returned her attention to me. "We need someone from Alstone High who's also neutral to help out."

"Uh. Maybe Milo's girlfriend? Katie?"

"Perfect. Get her number for me, and we'll get it sorted out."

Resting my head against the wall, I flashed her a grin. I was lucky to have her and Danny in my corner. "I fucking love you both, you know."

I'd left Talia to her planning, and a few days later, it was time to face the next test.

Meeting Levi's parents.

He'd asked to tell them about us on his own, worried about their reaction after what had happened with my mum, but they'd completely shocked him. His mum had told him that she'd always wondered if he was bisexual, and his dad, not at all helpfully, had shown his support by offering to set Levi up with his boss' gay son, some rich asshole by the name of Clifford, if things didn't work out between us. Thanks, but no thanks.

Then they'd asked to meet me, so here I was, standing outside their house and trying my very fucking hardest to stay calm. It was supposed to be a casual thing, just to introduce myself and stay for a quick drink, but even so, it was a big deal for both me and Levi.

Levi swung open the front door to find me shifting on my feet, clenching and unclenching my fists. "Don't be nervous. They'll like you."

"I'm not nervous." I followed him inside, closing the door behind me. Pausing for a second, I took a deep breath, straightening my shoulders. Then I stepped into the hallway.

"Ash." Levi stopped me, placing his hands on my shoulders and squeezing lightly as he pressed a soft kiss to my lips. "Remember, they've already accepted this. Us. Just be your usual charming-slash-annoying self, avoid mentioning the time you sprayed tequila all over the media room, and it'll be fine."

His words eased something inside me, and I slid my arms around his waist, hugging him to me. "Can I mention my knife?"

"*No.*"

"You're no fun." I gave him one last quick kiss before releasing him. "Let's do this, then."

He slid his fingers through mine and led me into a small room off the kitchen with large armchairs and a small sofa, where apparently his parents liked to relax when they were at home, preferring it to the cavernous lounge on the other side of the house.

"Mum, Dad. This is, uh, this is my Asher. Asher. Henderson. My boyfriend, Asher Henderson."

Seeing him suddenly nervous and tripping over his words eased my own nerves, and all I wanted was to reassure him. I realised then just how important this meeting was to him.

Making sure to look them both in the eye, I stuck out my hand to Levi's dad. He was tall with salt-and-pepper hair, and the same grey eyes as Levi. "Mr. Woodford. It's a pleasure."

Shaking my hand firmly, he gave me a genuine smile. "The pleasure is ours. We've been hearing a lot about you from Levi."

I turned to Levi's mum, a tiny, stylishly dressed woman with ash-brown hair and light blue eyes. "Mrs. Woodford." Taking her hand, I kissed the back of it, ignoring Levi's amused snort. What? I had manners. He'd just never seen them in action before. "Thank you so much for having me."

"We've been so excited to meet Levi's boyfriend," she confided, giving me a huge smile, and I completely relaxed. "Anyone who can make our son as happy as he's been lately…well, I've been very curious about the person who put a smile on his face."

I didn't even have to look at Levi to know that he was embarrassed—I could practically feel it radiating from him. Curling my fingers around his, I slid my thumb back and forth over his hand while his dad got to work on making everyone drinks, and his mum directed us to sit on the sofa.

"Thanks," he whispered, too low for them to hear, pressing his thigh against mine.

"So, Asher." Mrs. Woodford treated me to another warm smile. "You must tell me the name of your hairstylist. Are they local? I only ask because your hair looks almost identical to one of the male model's I worked with during my last ad campaign in France. I've been trying to find a stylist here who can recreate that kind of artfully dishevelled, effortless look for another campaign."

"Mum! Are you blind?" Levi stared at her in disbelief, while I couldn't hold in my laughter. She stared between us both, her eyes dancing with humour and curiosity.

"Let me explain," I said when I eventually had my laughter under control. "Levi's under the deluded impression that my hair's a hopeless mess."

"Levison, I hope you haven't been giving your poor boyfriend grief about his hair," Mr. Woodford cut in, to my amusement. This was fucking hilarious, and I knew it would be something I made sure I reminded Levi of on a regular basis in the future.

"I don't believe this," he muttered, shaking his head, but there was a smile tugging at the corners of his lips. I knew he loved my hair, really. It had to be jealousy that I didn't spend ages in front of the mirror getting it to look just right. That wasn't to say I didn't appreciate the effort he made. I did. Very much. My boyfriend was hot as fuck.

"To answer your question, I don't have a stylist. I get it cut at the local barber's in Highnam. Other than that, I wash it, and it just dries like this." I shrugged, giving Mrs. Woodford a smile.

"You're very lucky." Returning my smile, she leaned forwards in her chair. "Now, tell me. Would you like to join us for a family dinner on Sunday?"

I glanced over at Levi, and he gave me a huge smile, so full of relief and happiness that there was no way I was going to decline the invitation.

"I'd love to."

TWENTY-SIX
LEVI

"It's only been two weeks. Give her time."

Asher's dark brows pulled together, his mouth twisting as he met my gaze through the phone screen. "Yeah, I know. I know." He lifted a mug to his lips, steam curling from the top, before continuing. "I think she's started to thaw a bit. At least she's stopped saying that me and Talia suited each other so well and we should work things out, never mind that she's with Danny now, and neither of us are into each other."

All I could do to reassure him was to tell him what I hoped was true. "Listen, Ash. Your mum loves you, and she'll eventually realise this isn't an experimental phase."

"Yeah. You're here to stay." His eyes softened, before he sighed. "I wish she wouldn't change the subject when I bring you up in conversation, though. It really fucking hurts, to be honest."

I hated this. Hated that he was hurting and I wasn't there. I just wanted to hug him, but right now he was in Highnam and I was at home in Alstone. At least I'd see him soon.

As far as everything else went, things were improving. At Alstone High, the football team had put out the word that if anyone else tried to mess with anyone from Highnam Academy, the whole team would rain hell down on them. Since we had so much popularity, and therefore power, no one had stepped out of line. Asher had done the same at Highnam Academy, too, and things had mostly simmered down.

"I know it hurts. I wish I could make it better."

He smiled at me, and it reached his eyes. "You do."

There was a knock at the media room door, and Milo appeared in the doorway. I waved him in, then turned back to Asher. "Milo's here now."

"Alright. See you in a couple of hours?"

We said our goodbyes and then I flopped back on the sofa with a groan.

"Why can't people just accept that me and Ash want to be together?"

I wasn't really asking a question, but Milo answered anyway as he took a seat in the gaming chair. "It hasn't been as bad as you thought it would be, has it? It's got to be hard enough convincing people you're over the whole rivalry, and adding a relationship when you've both been straight up to this point, as far as anyone knows... But no one's really given you that much trouble, have they?"

"No...I'm mostly talking about Asher's mum. It feels like she might be slowly coming round to the idea of me and him together, but it fucking kills me when I see him getting upset about it."

"Oh, yeah, that sucks." He stretched his legs out in front of him, rocking back in the chair. "I guess all you can do is give it time."

"Yeah."

His phone beeped with a message alert, and he glanced down at the screen. "Katie. Reminding me that we need to be at the pitch by eleven. The level of organisation between her and Talia...it's kind of scary."

I laughed. "You're not wrong there." Katie and Talia hadn't even met in person yet, but somehow they'd managed to organise this entire thing together, and get everyone on board, all within a ridiculously short space of time. Katie had also pulled some strings with the local media, thanks to her dad's connections, and the result of all their scheming was a plan to show everyone that Alstone High and Highnam Academy were over the animosity. Today was the day we were putting it into place.

"It'll be worth it, though." Leaning forwards, Milo grabbed one of the game controllers. "Want a game before we go?"

Picking up my own controller, I shot him a grin. "Yes."

ASHER

Stepping through the park gates, I tugged the sleeves of my hoodie down over my hands to try and chase away the chill in my fingers. Here we were, carrying out Talia and Katie's plan, which involved Alstone's and Highnam's football teams. It was a cold December day, and we were set to freeze our fucking balls off at one of Parton Park's public football pitches, playing a friendly training match with mixed teams.

All of us. As in, every single member of both teams.

It was completely unbelievable that something like this was actually happening, because I could guarantee that not one of us would have come up with an idea like this, let alone actually want to carry it out, but Talia and Katie were apparently running the show.

As I'd agreed with Levi beforehand, I'd turned up early along with Danny so that he could meet Milo. Officially—since the first time they'd met hadn't been under the best of circumstances, what with me being all battered and bruised. Talia and Katie had shown up early too, since they were organising the whole thing, although they were giving us space. They were off at the side of the pitch, looking at something or other on a clipboard, leaving the four of us alone.

As we made our way towards the goalposts where Levi and Milo were waiting, I glanced over at Danny. "Be nice, please. This means a lot to me."

He rolled his eyes. "Yeah, alright."

I slowed my pace, dragging my feet, my football boots crunching on the frosty ground.

A heavy sigh came from him. "Ash. I know what he means to you. I'm not gonna be a dick about it, okay?"

"I know." And I did. Danny was my best mate, and I knew that he'd come through for me. When the news of me and Levi had spread, a few bigoted fucks had a problem with my sexual orientation, and…let's just say, you didn't want to piss him off. My best mate had ended up being my biggest supporter, like I knew he would. I'd do the same for him. We had each other's backs.

I couldn't seem to stop this fucking nervous feeling inside me, though.

Danny shot me a sideways look. "You know that you're only stressing because this is the first time you're meeting Milo without hostility, don't you? Y'know, since he's your boyfriend's best mate and all. You want to make a good impression, am I right?"

Fuck. Yeah. He was totally right.

I guess I owed the guy an apology for pulling a knife on him.

When we reached the goalposts, though, I only had eyes for one person. I stepped straight up to my boyfriend, who had a wide smile on his face. An answering smile curved over my lips as I took him in. "Hi."

He dragged me closer, placing a quick kiss to my mouth, and then slid his fingers through mine. "Hi."

Keeping my grip on Levi's hand, I turned my attention to his best friend, who was eyeing me warily. "So. Milo. I guess I owe you an apology for the whole knife thing."

I ignored Danny's snort of amusement, keeping my focus on Milo. He remained silent for a minute, studying me, then a wry smile twisted his mouth. "I did come at you in the alley." His gaze flicked to Levi, then back, his brown eyes meeting mine. Holding out his hand to me, he raised his brows. "What do you say we start over? I hear from Levi that you're not so bad, you know, when you're not threatening people with knives."

Next to me, I felt Levi relax, and I stroked my thumb across his skin in what I hoped was a reassuring movement. "Alright. Same deal with Danny?" I inclined my head towards Danny, who had come to stand on my other side. Milo nodded, we all shook hands, and that was that.

"My turn." Danny stepped around me, holding out his hand to Levi. "Don't hurt my best mate, and we won't have any problems."

"Deal." Levi gave him a short nod, they shook hands, and I huffed out a relieved breath. That had all been relatively painless.

"You okay?" Levi spoke low in my ear, tugging me back into him, and I nodded. Over by Talia and Katie, the rest of the teams were beginning to arrive. While they knew about our relationship now, I knew some of them were struggling to make sense of it all. I wanted all our focus to be on the training session today, so after giving Levi a quick kiss, I squeezed his hand and then let him go. "Yeah. I'm good. I guess it's time to put this plan into action."

After greeting everyone, we split into two teams and lined up on the pitch, each team a mix of Highnam Academy and Alstone High players. There were a few hostile looks between some of the players, but the atmosphere was generally positive. Talia blew the whistle, and then we began.

By the end of the time period, it seemed like the plan might have worked. Both teams had honestly shocked me by playing well together, and the journalist and photographer from the local paper, snapping pictures and pulling various team members aside for sound bites, had loved every minute of it. The idea was that if we showed that there was no animosity between the two teams, through this completely contrived "training session," complete with photo evidence and an article to back it up, then people would believe it. Not only that, but bringing both teams together in this way was good for everyone involved, since there'd been so much bad blood thanks to everything that had gone down between us.

I hoped we'd done enough to put out the fire, but after

our publicity stunt came the real test. Alstone High was due to face Highnam Academy in a championship match, and this time, Highnam had the home advantage.

TWENTY-SEVEN
ASHER

It was the day of reckoning.

When the teams filed out onto the pitch, the roar from the crowd was deafening in its intensity. Last time we'd played each other, it had ended up with Highnam losing 4-0, and I knew Alstone High wouldn't go easy on us today, despite our more friendly status. As it should be—there was no honour in beating someone who let you win.

Both teams lined up on the field, and as we'd agreed beforehand, every team member went down the line, making a point of shaking the hand of the opposing players. When I got to Levi, he returned my grin, his thumb lightly stroking over my hand as he gripped it.

Then it was time. Both teams faced each other as the referee held up the coin. Grey eyes met mine, just like the last time. Except now, there was no hostility in Levi's gaze.

Get ready to lose, Seven, I mouthed.

A smile tugged at his lips. *Fuck you, Ten*, he mouthed back, exactly as he'd done before.

Afterwards, I returned, watching with satisfaction as his eyes flashed with barely concealed lust before he schooled his expression.

The coin toss went in Alstone High's favour, and then I had no time to think about anything else except the game.

Dave and Mick barked instructions from the sidelines as we took off. I grinned as I booted the ball down the pitch towards Danny, the grass crunching under my feet and the icy breeze chilling my face. No matter what other shit happened, football was the one thing that was a constant in my life. Win or lose, I loved this game.

There were two yellow cards given in the first half, both to Highnam Academy players, but I was proud of my boys—they had some angry words for the ref but didn't show any outward animosity towards the Alstone High players involved.

When it was half-time, the score was 1-0 to Alstone High, but I knew we could win this. Both teams were evenly matched, both out to win, but we were playing better than we ever had done. If we could keep it together, the match could be ours. I said as much to the team once Dave and Mick had given their usual pep talk.

"They may have scored the first goal, but we're gonna win this. Dan, their left side's looking weak. We need to take advantage. Remember what Jones was like when we played that fake training game for the article"—huh, maybe it had helped in a way I hadn't anticipated—"and use it. Get past him, and I know we can score from there."

After a few final comments from Dave and Mick to wrap it up, we filed back onto the pitch, ready to win.

The atmosphere was electric, and it spurred us on. Less than five minutes into the second half, Jim, one of our strikers, sent the ball curving into the back of the net. Their goalie never even stood a chance of stopping it. Seven minutes after that, I crossed the ball to Danny, who took advantage of Alstone High's weaker left side, chipping the ball into the goal and putting us in the lead for the first time during the match.

Now we just had to hold on to it and not let Alstone High score. The countdown of the clock seemed endless, faces becoming a blur, Highnam working together to deflect attack after attack from Alstone High.

Somehow we made it to the end of the ninety minutes, and then there were just two minutes of added time to get through. Two more minutes to hold on to our lead.

The whole crowd seemed to hold their breath as Milo sent the ball straight over the heads of our defenders, right at the top corner of the net. It seemed to happen in slow motion—Omar, our goalie, lunged to the side, his arms outstretched, and by some miracle, the tips of his fingers connected with the ball.

It was deflected, and then ten seconds later, the final whistle blew, and it was all over.

We'd done it.

Highnam Academy had won the match.

As the crowds went crazy and my team celebrated around me, I jogged over to Levi, making a point of shaking his hand.

"You played well out there."

He gave me a wry smile. "Not quite well enough, but you deserved to win. Good game."

I lowered my voice. "I know *exactly* how to cheer you up later. I'm gonna make sure you score with me."

"I'm holding you to that." His eyes glimmered with

amusement and lust, and I couldn't wait to get him alone.

There was no more time to talk now, though. Celebrations came first. The stands were already beginning to empty out, so as we'd collectively agreed earlier, both teams made a point of shaking hands before we left the field, offering congratulations and commiserations to each other. We'd done all we could now, and based on the reaction of the crowds, it looked like it might have been enough. Maybe we could finally put this rivalry behind us and go back to the way things used to be.

An hour later, Levi's McLaren pulled up outside the front of the mostly empty school. My teammates had disappeared to celebrate our win, and I'd join them later, but right now I needed to see my boyfriend. When he climbed out of his car, I headed straight over to him, crowding him against the side of the car and kissing his smiling mouth. His arms came around me, and when we drew apart, both of us were breathless.

"Hi." I angled my head to run my teeth along the line of his jaw, and he shivered.

"Mmm. Hi."

"Ready for your consolation prize?" Grinding my hips into his, I kissed down his throat, leaving him with no doubt of my intentions.

"Ash, wait." His tone had me instantly curious, and I raised my head, meeting his gaze.

"What?"

"You won the match, so I guess you can have your reward." Taking my hand, he straightened out my palm. "Here."

I stared at the object he'd placed in my hand in shock, and then my eyes flew to his. "Are you serious?"

"Yeah, I'm serious." He grinned at me, enjoying my surprise. "But don't make me regret it. I don't even want a scratch on it."

"You're actually going to let me drive your precious car?" I ran my fingers over the smooth black key. "You must really love me."

The words came out without any thought, and as soon as I said them, I cringed.

"I mean—"

He pulled me into him, lightly biting down on my bottom lip, then slanting his mouth over mine. I felt the tremor in his body as I tightened my arms around him, and the moment became completely overwhelming.

I *knew*.

"Yeah, I do. I do love you," he breathed against my lips. "Really, really love you."

"Oh, fuck," I mumbled, dipping my head to his neck, burying my face like I did when it all became too much.

His huff of amusement was followed by a kiss to my hair. "You're ridiculous sometimes."

"But you love me."

"Yeah."

Finally gathering my courage, I raised my head, meeting his eyes. I was Asher Henderson, for fuck's sake. It shouldn't be so scary to say the words back to him when I meant them with every single part of me.

He gave me a soft smile, and suddenly, I wasn't scared anymore.

Holding his gaze, I returned his smile. "Levi Samuel Woodford. I love you."

A laugh burst out of him, his grey eyes shining silver. "That's not my middle name."

Grinning, I slid my hands down his back and onto his ass. "It's not my fault your real middle name is completely unpronounceable."

"I know what your middle name is. Dickhead."

"Yep, you definitely love me." I slid my lips over his, then pulled out of his arms. "Are you gonna let me drive this car or what?"

"I'm already regretting this."

When I was positioned in the driver's seat with my slightly apprehensive-looking boyfriend next to me, I leaned over the centre console, kissing the side of his face. "I really do love you, Levi."

He turned his head, capturing my mouth, his hand coming up to grip my jaw as he kissed me, hot and slow and deep. "I know. Show me how much you love me by not crashing my car, okay?"

I started the engine with a roar, euphoria thrumming through my entire body.

"You might wanna hold on to something."

Then I hit the accelerator.

TWENTY-EIGHT
LEVI

FOUR MONTHS LATER

We were halfway through the Easter break, and things between me and Asher were going from strength to strength. Asher's mum had extended an invitation for me to join her and Asher for dinner on Easter Sunday, which was huge, because it had taken her a long time to come round to the idea of Asher being in a committed relationship with a man.

It had taken a while for all our friends to get used to being around each other, too, but we were getting there. My media room had somehow become the designated neutral territory, aka a gathering place for mine and Asher's combined friendship groups. In here, there was an unspoken agreement that we didn't mention schools, or the rivalry, or anything like that.

Right now, Milo, Katie, and my teammates, Carl and Jack, were in the middle of a card game with Danny and

Talia, while Asher's teammate, Omar, was playing darts with Neveah, one of Katie's friends from our school.

As for me, I was sprawled across the middle of the large sofa, with Asher leaning against the side armrest, his legs kicked up over mine, both of us mashing our controllers as our characters fought on-screen.

"Fighting you always makes me wanna fuck," Asher said in a low voice when our current round was over.

I slid my hand up his thigh, dangerously close to his crotch, what with us being in a roomful of people. "I know. Me too." A thought occurred to me. "We're not talking about fighting in this game, are we?"

He laughed, his gaze flicking to the screen that now showed our characters posing in various fighting stances. "No way. I was just thinking about it. Us." His laughter died away. Shifting in his seat, he stared at me from beneath his lashes.

"Ash...don't look at me like that."

"Like what?"

How one person's smile could be so innocent and so evil at the same time, I had no idea. It was a skill.

"Okay! Fifteen minutes and everyone needs to leave," I announced loudly to the room in general.

Asher kicked me.

"Ten minutes!"

Groans of protest echoed around the room, but because they were good friends, they didn't complain too much. We'd all been hanging out here for the past few hours, anyway. Now it was getting late, my boyfriend was horny, and I wanted him to ride my dick.

When they'd finally left us alone, I shut the door firmly. My parents weren't here, and Asher and I had the place to ourselves. I wasn't going to waste the opportunity.

Neither was he.

The second the door had clicked shut, sealing us inside, the atmosphere in the room flipped, growing heavy with anticipation.

"Remember how I said fighting you makes me wanna fuck? Even *thinking* about fighting you seems to have the same effect." Lifting himself off the sofa, he met my gaze, his brown eyes almost black with his huge pupils, his lips parted, and his chest heaving as he stared at me. He lifted his T-shirt and, in one smooth movement, ripped it over his head, leaving him in his low-slung sweatpants that did absolutely fucking nothing to hide the large outline of his hardening cock.

"Fucking *hell*," I groaned, my dick instantly responding to the sight of him, thickening in my loose shorts, the fabric tenting obscenely. I yanked my own shirt off, and time stopped for a second, both of us frozen in place.

Then he lunged for me.

When his body slammed into mine, sending me crashing into the wall and knocking the breath from my lungs, I was stunned for a second, but my reflexes kicked in. I twisted out of his hold, getting a grip around his waist and throwing us both to the floor.

As we rolled, knocking into the back of the sofa, he managed to get me pinned under him, grabbing a handful of my hair and yanking my head back, his mouth going to my throat. He sucked hard, using his teeth, grinding his hard cock against me as he left his mark on my skin.

"Asher, *fuck*," I moaned, thrusting up against him, shoving my hands under the waistband of his sweatpants and digging the pads of my fingers into his muscular ass.

He lifted his head from my throat to slam his mouth down on mine, teeth and lips and tongue, rolling us again without breaking the connection. Now I had the upper hand, and as our mouths tore apart, I twisted my legs around his. Relinquishing my grip on his ass to pin his hands down against the floor, I lowered my head, leaving a chain of biting kisses along his jaw. He panted beneath me, finally wrestling his hands free and, with a sudden twist, broke free of my hold. Springing to his feet, he vaulted over the side of the sofa, landing on his feet, facing me.

"Come and get me, baby." He gave me a wild grin, his eyes bright with excitement and a heady lust that made my dick jump.

My voice was a low, rasped warning. "You'd better run."

He held his position until I rounded the corner, almost in reach of him, then feinted to the left. I could read him so well by this point that I blocked his movement, swiping his legs out from under him with my own as we both crashed back onto the sofa.

I struggled to a seated position, tugging him up with me.

Breathing hard, he moved to straddle me, his knees on either side of my thighs, and his hands planted either side of my head, gripping onto the back of the sofa.

"Do you give in?" He rolled his hips down, his face lowered to mine, his breath ghosting across my lips.

"Never." My hands slid back into his sweatpants, down over his ass. "Do you?"

"Never." Leaving one of his hands braced on the back of the sofa, he brought the other one down to grip my jaw, angling my head. He licked a long, slow stripe up the tendon of my throat, stopping at the top. Releasing me, he mouthed at my jaw while his hand ran down over my chest, the pads of his fingers rubbing over my nipples.

"Ash," I gasped, thrusting up into him, needing the friction. It was almost too much. My cock was dripping precum, rock-hard and throbbing.

His fingers mapped out the lines of my body, down over the ridges of my abs, and stopped at the band of my shorts.

"Don't stop." My hips bucked up as he ground down. "We need to be naked. I need to feel your cock against mine."

"Fuck. Yessss."

Sliding down to the floor, he tugged off my shorts. I hadn't bothered with underwear, and my cock sprung free. His face was so close that I could feel his hot breath on my thighs, and I groaned as he wrapped his hand around the base of my hard length. His tongue darted out to lick his lips, and then he tilted his head forwards. "I fucking love your cock." One swipe of his tongue, followed by his hot, wet mouth closing over the head, and I was fucking undone.

"Ash, fuck. No. I won't last." I tugged at his hair urgently, and he released me with an obscene pop, swiping his tongue across his lips, catching the bead of precum on his bottom lip.

He climbed to his feet, his hands going to the waistband of his sweatpants. "You wanna fill me with your cock, baby?"

"*Yes.*"

The desperation was clear in my tone, and he didn't waste any more time, ridding himself of the rest of his clothes, his thick cock jutting out from his body, his muscles tense and flexing as my gaze licked all over him.

"I need you now."

Crouching down, he reached for the lube that I'd stashed under the sofa earlier, drizzling a generous amount over his fingers, and then kneeling back in front of me, he stroked his hands up and down in a twisting motion, coating my dick. I bit down on my lip hard enough for the pain to distract me from the pleasure, digging my fingers into my palms until my nails made indents in the skin.

"You know when we were in the shower earlier and you were driving me fucking crazy with your tongue and your fingers?" He released my throbbing cock, climbing back onto the sofa to straddle me.

I made a choked noise in my throat. Rimming him under the waterfall head, his cum hitting the walls of the shower as his thighs shook against my shoulders…I did *not* need that visual when I was already on the brink.

"And you know that certain item you bought when we did all those tequila shots? I didn't wanna waste all your effort in the shower, so I might have been using it on myself until about twenty minutes ago, when I removed it."

"Asher. Stop. Talking. And. Let. Me. Fuck. You." My jaw was clenched so painfully that I could feel my teeth grinding together, and I couldn't even handle the thought of him using the plug we'd drunkenly ordered on himself.

"Yeah, I'm gonna let you." He grasped the base of my cock and slid himself down, impaling himself on my hard length. Even with his preparations, he was so fucking tight that I had to stop him when he was fully on me, gripping onto his thighs and taking long inhales and exhales through my nose, desperately trying to regain control. His cock was hard between us, smearing precum over my skin, and his ass flexed around my dick even though he wasn't moving. We'd stopped using condoms a couple of months earlier after getting tested, and the feel of my cock inside him right now, with nothing between us, was almost too much to handle.

"Come here." I released my grip on his thighs, sliding

my hand up his back to the nape of his neck. "Kiss me."

His mouth met mine, hot and hungry, our kisses turning messy as he began to move against me, moaning into my mouth. "You feel so fucking good," he rasped, his powerful thighs flexing as he rolled his hips, his cock jerking against my stomach. "You wanna lie down?"

"Yeah," I breathed, and the next second, he was angling us round so that I was lying on my back lengthways on the huge sofa, while he rode my dick.

"So...fucking...good." His movements grew more erratic, and I knew he was close, knew my dick was hitting him in just the right place with every move he made. Thrusting up as he thrust down, I wrapped my hand around his cock, and then he was coming, shuddering against my body, tightening around my dick as he threw his head back, his throat working as he groaned out his orgasm.

When he'd come down from his high, he angled his body forwards, sliding his fingers through mine. He stared down at me, all kiss-swollen lips, mussed hair, and huge pupils as he continued to ride my dick, up and down, in a relentless rhythm, driving me closer and closer to the edge. "Fuck...Levi. If you could see yourself now. You're so fucking hot."

Already on the edge for so long, I dropped, free-falling into the most intense orgasm I'd ever had in my life, coming so hard that my entire body was shaking, my vision going black as Asher rode me through the aftershocks.

When I'd recovered enough to pry my eyes open, I curled my arm around Asher, who had crawled up my body to lie sprawled out over me, placing soft, lazy kisses on whatever parts of me he could reach without moving.

"I think we should just sleep in here tonight." He yawned

against my skin, and I guess it was contagious, because a yawn overtook me.

"No way." As much as I didn't want to move, I knew we'd regret it in the morning if we didn't. "Come on. Quick clean-up in the shower, then you can lie all over me in my nice, comfortable bed, where we have room to spread out without you hanging off the side."

"If we must." He pouted, making me laugh.

"Ash, you're half hanging off this sofa. You don't want to end up on the floor, do you?"

"Yeah, alright." He pressed another kiss to the side of my jaw before clambering off the sofa. "I guess it'll be more comfortable."

When we'd eventually dragged ourselves upstairs, in and out of the shower, and crawled under my bedcovers, my eyes were already half-closed.

His heavy weight wrapped around me as he threw his leg across mine, his arm draped across my chest. "Remember the first time you got me on your bed?" he asked, his voice thick with sleep. "I wanted you so much, even then."

I turned my head to kiss him, a soft, slow slide of his lips against mine. "Yeah. I wanted you too."

"And now you have me." He shifted closer, and my arm curved around his back.

"And you have me."

My bedroom was dark, but I felt his smile against my lips. "I love you so much."

"I love you, too." Lying here, with the warmth of his body pressed against me, knowing that he'd be the first thing I saw in the morning when I woke, I smiled. We'd started out as rivals, and it had been a rough journey at times, but it had been totally worth it to get to where we were today. Asher was it for me. When you found your soulmate, no matter how young or old you were, you knew—and I knew with everything in me that he was the person I wanted to spend the rest of my life with. And I knew it was the same for him.

I let my eyes close, happy.

EPILOGUE
ASHER

SEVEN YEARS LATER

After greeting Phil, Levi's boss, I made my way down to Levi's office, where he worked as a car designer. His official title was Automotive Design Engineer, but basically, he got to design cars alongside a team of other designers and then see his visions come to life. He was engrossed in something on his computer screen, so I stopped in the open doorway and took a second to take him in.

I was a lucky, lucky man. Levi was fucking gorgeous. Right now, his toned body was encased in a fitted navy suit, and he had his bottom lip tugged between his teeth as he stared at the screen, his brows pulled together in concentration.

When he raised his head and his eyes met mine, a smile spread across his face. He was out of his chair and over to me before I had a chance to speak, his arms coming around my waist.

"Hi," he murmured against my lips before stealing a kiss that took my breath away. I slid my arms around him, deepening the kiss, stroking my tongue into his mouth as he backed me up against the wall of his office.

"Mmm. My favourite way to be greeted, by my favourite person in the world," I said when we finally broke apart.

Levi's gaze went all soft as he smiled at me. "My favourite, too. I love you so much."

"You're gonna love me even more in a minute." Reaching into my pocket, my fingers closed around the thin pieces of card. Pulling them out, I handed them to him. "Happy anniversary. I love you."

"You got us tickets for the FA Cup Final? I thought they were all sold out." He stared down at the tickets in disbelief.

"They were, but I have connections." Grinning at his raised brow, I elaborated. "You know, from my job. I wasn't sure if I'd be able to get hold of them, even so, but Tony came through for me." Working as a football coach for a Premier League youth team had its benefits, and based on the look on Levi's face, he was definitely appreciative of those benefits. I hadn't had the job for long, since before that I'd been working with a team in a lower division, but I was already reaping the rewards.

"Your job is the best." Stepping away from me, Levi returned to his computer. "Give me a second to shut this down, then I'll give you your anniversary present."

"I'm not sure you wanna be caught fucking me at work, after what happened last time."

He shook his head, amusement shining in his eyes. "Ash. That's not your present." Switching off his monitor, he returned to me and placed a soft kiss to my lips. His hands slid down to my ass as he pulled me into him. "But I'm *definitely* going to be doing that later."

"Yeah, you are." I tugged his lip between my teeth, feeling him shiver against me.

"How is it I want you so much, all the time?" Releasing his grip on my ass, he grabbed my hand. "Come on, let's go down to the workshop before we end up doing something that could get me fired."

"I want you all the time, too, just so you know."

"I know." Pushing open the door to the corridor that led to the workshop, he gave me a grin. "We'll make the most of that later. But now..." Trailing off, he increased his pace, pulling me with him. He paused outside the workshop doors. "I think you're going to like this."

The excitement in his eyes was contagious. "Show me." I placed my hand over the button to open the doors.

"Wait. No jewellery allowed in the workshop, remember."

"Oh, yeah." Taking Levi's left hand, I lifted it, placing a kiss to his palm before sliding the chunky platinum wedding band off his ring finger, revealing the small tattoo hidden underneath. A number ten—a reminder of how we'd started out when we were eighteen and how far we'd come. A reminder of me, forever inked into his skin.

He took my hand and did the same, and my own tattoo was exposed. Number seven. My own permanent reminder of the person I loved with every part of me, the man who I got to share the rest of my life with. His lips slid softly over the ink before he pocketed both rings with a smile. "Now, you can have your present."

We entered the huge workshop, all polished steel and tinted glass, and Levi moved in front of me, blocking my view. His hand came up to cover my eyes. "Don't look."

"I don't have much choice since you're covering my eyes."

With a soft laugh, he moved around behind me, keeping one hand over my eyes, his other sliding around my waist. He shuffled us forwards, then stopped, his lips brushing over my ear as he dipped his head. "Happy anniversary, Asher Henderson-Woodford."

Then he dropped his hand, and I found myself staring at a car, all low, sleek lines and shiny silver paintwork. It looked like a cross between a high-end sports car and some kind of futuristic spaceship. It was a fucking work of art.

"This is the concept car I've been working on," he said, almost shyly. "I thought you might want to take it for its inaugural drive round the track."

There was a lump in my throat. "This is the one you were the lead designer on?" I spun in his arms, my hands sliding up his back. "You... Your talent seriously blows me away."

"Yeah." His smile was soft, and I couldn't help kissing him.

"I love you so much. I can't even—Levi." Burying my head in his shoulder, I tightened my grip on him. He placed a kiss to my hair.

"I love you, Ash. I know this isn't something you can keep, but you get to drive it around the track. And I might have pulled some strings of my own with my work connections."

When I raised my head to meet his gaze, his eyes were shining, and his smile was wide and bright.

"You know who won the Formula 1 Grand Prix last year? He might just be out there on the track, ready to race against you."

"Are you fucking serious?" I stared at him, wide-eyed. "How did you manage that?"

"I told you. My connections. Well, that, and the fact that my team's working on a new prototype race car for him, so I managed to persuade him to do me this favour while he was here to check out the progress we've made." Dropping a quick kiss on my lips, he stepped back. "He won't be driving a Formula 1 car, by the way. He's going to be driving one of our normal cars to make it a fairer race. Oh, also—there's a speed limiter on both cars, because they wouldn't agree to us doing it otherwise. But I know you'll make it a good race, even so." With that, he headed over to the huge doors that opened out onto the short road that led to the racetrack, where they tested the new cars.

After opening the doors, he came back over to me. "Ready?"

"Fuck, yeah. I was born ready."

When I was seated inside the car, racing harness on and a helmet on my head— "just in case, our insurance makes us take these precautions" —I looked up at Levi. "Are you getting in?"

"You want me with you?"

"Yeah, I do. Always."

Two spins around the track and I was used to the feel of the car, enough that I was ready to race. Pulling up to the start line, I watched a low-slung black car roll up next to me, the driver flashing me a thumbs up. This whole moment was so surreal—I was about to race against an actual Formula 1 champion. And even better, I got to experience this moment with Levi.

"You can beat him." Levi squeezed my hand before

releasing it to place his palm on my thigh.

I smiled at the man I loved. "Doesn't matter if I beat him or not. Just the fact that I'm getting to do something that only a handful of people have ever done, in a car my talented as fuck husband designed... Plus, there's no shame in losing to the world champion."

"That's true." He laughed, then his eyes met mine. "As much as I'm looking forward to this, I'm looking forward to what comes after even more. You and me, in our huge bed in our new Chelsea flat, celebrating our anniversary in my favourite way."

"Mmm. Not just in the bed. The shower, too—we need to make the most of it. You could fit five people in there."

"I don't want five people. Just you, Asher."

My heart was so fucking full. "Same. Only ever you." Leaning across the centre of the car, I gave him a soft kiss, our helmets bumping together.

Then I settled back into my seat, watching the clock overhead, waiting for it to count down to zero and for the red light to turn green. I repeated the words I'd said to him on the day he let me drive his McLaren for the first time. A day that I knew neither of us would ever forget, because it was the day we'd first told each other that we loved each other, back when we were eighteen.

"You might wanna hold on to something."

As I hit the accelerator and we went flying down the track, neck and neck with the black car, his answering laugh was wild and exhilarated.

A huge smile spread across my face.

Life was good.

THE END

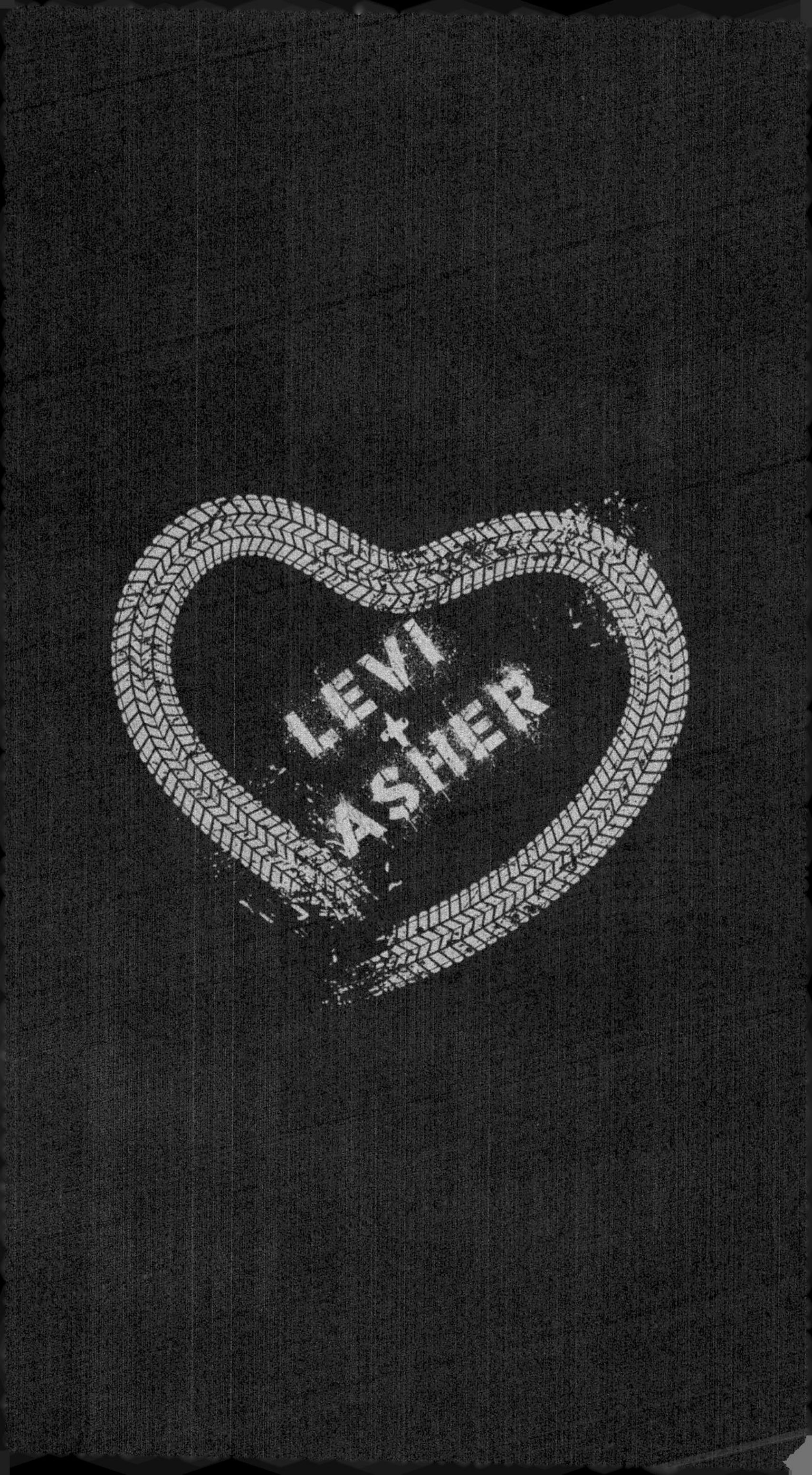
LEVI
+
ASHER

THANK YOU

Thank you so much for reading Asher and Levi's story!

Feel free to send me your thoughts, and reviews are always very appreciated. You can find me in my Facebook group Becca's Book Bar if you want to connect, or sign up to my newsletter to stay up to date with all the latest info. Check out all my links at
https://linktr.ee/authorbeccasteele

Want more M/M from Alstone High? Get Cross the Line now, available on Kindle Unlimited at
http://mybook.to/ctl

Becca xoxo

ACKNOWLEDGEMENTS

First of all I have to thank Kelly, who encouraged me to write this, and gave me valuable feedback on the story! You're awesome!

I also need to thank Jenny, Jen, and Megan, for all the support you give me, and for your feedback on this story. Thanks as well to Sandra and Rumi for editing and proofreading—especially for putting up with my last minute sliding into your emails with files. I swear I will be better organised one day. Just not yet.

Thanks to Danielle, Steffanie, and the others involved in the Brutal Boys anthology where this book first appeared. And to the other authors who wrote with me and encouraged me—Ivy, Tracy, Chelsea, Ramzi, Veronica, Rachel, and so many others who have encouraged and inspired me! And of course, Claudia, who not only encouraged and supported me but had to deal with me bugging her with a million different ideas for the cover. Speaking of the cover, a huge thanks to Michelle and Andy for the gorgeous image!

To Wildfire, GRR, my street team, ARC team, and all the bloggers and bookstagrammers—I appreciate the reads, reviews, promo, edits…you do an amazing job every day!

Finally, thank you so much for taking the time to pick up this book and read Asher and Levi's story.

Becca xoxo

P.S. An extra huge thank you to Jon & Simon. You know why. Gin is on its way!

ABOUT THE AUTHOR

Becca Steele is a USA Today and Wall Street Journal bestselling romance author. She currently lives in the south of England with her husband, two kids, and a whole horde of characters that reside inside her head.

When she's not writing, you can find her reading or watching Netflix, usually with a glass of wine in hand. Failing that, she'll be online hunting for memes, or wasting time making her 500th Spotify playlist.

Join Becca's Facebook reader group Becca's Book Bar, sign up to her mailing list, or find her via the following links:

www.authorbeccasteele.com
www.facebook.com/authorbeccasteele
www.instagram.com/authorbeccasteele
www.goodreads.com/authorbeccasteele

ALSO BY BECCA STEELE

The Four Series
The Lies We Tell
The Secrets We Hide
The Havoc We Wreak
A Cavendish Christmas (free short story)*
The Fight In Us
The Bonds We Break

Alstone High Standalones
Trick Me Twice
Cross the Line (M/M)
In a Week (free short story)*
Savage Rivals (M/M)

London Players Series
The Offer

London Suits Series
The Deal
The Truce
The Wish

Other Standalones
Mayhem (a Four Series spinoff)*

Boneyard Kings Series (with C. Lymari)
Merciless Kings (RH)

*all free short stories and bonus scenes are available from https://authorbeccasteele.com

Printed in Great Britain
by Amazon